During three decades as a writer, Gore Vidal's career has been marked by success and distinction. As a novelist, playwright and essayist his work has won international acclaim. He has also been an outspoken political activist. As a Democratic candidate for Congress from upstate New York, he received more votes there than any other Democrat in half a century.

He came to national attention in 1948 with the widely praised, widely condemned novel *The City and the Pillar*, the first American work to deal sympathetically with homosexuality. In the next six years he produced *The Judgment of Paris* and the prophetic *Messiah*.

After a hiatus to write films and plays, Vidal returned to the novel, creating three number one bestsellers in succession: *Julian*, *Washington, D.C.*, and *Myra Breckinridge*. Since 1973 he has produced a collection of essays, *Homage to Daniel Shays*, his highly esteemed novels *Burr*, *1876*, and the acclaimed bestseller *Kalki*.

Also by Gore Vidal
Published by Ballantine Books:

WASHINGTON, D.C.

1876

MYRON

DARK GREEN, BRIGHT RED

THE JUDGMENT OF PARIS

A SEARCH FOR THE KING

Williwaw

Gore Vidal

BALLANTINE BOOKS • NEW YORK

ISBN 0-345-25317-5

Originally published by E. P. Dutton & Company, Inc.

Manufactured in the United States of America

First Ballantine Books Edition: May 1978

For Nina

NOTE: *Williwaw is the Indian word for a big wind peculiar to the Aleutian islands and the Alaskan coast. It is a strong wind that sweeps suddenly down from the mountains toward the sea. The word williwaw, however, is now generally used to describe any big and sudden wind. It is in this last and more colloquial sense that I have used the term.*

G.V.

Chapter One

i

SOMEONE turned on the radio in the wheelhouse. A loud and sentimental song awakened him. He lay there for a moment in his bunk and stared at the square window in the wall opposite him. A sea gull flew lazily by the window. He watched it glide back and forth until it was out of sight.

He yawned and became conscious of an ache behind his eyes. There had been a party, he remembered. He felt sick. The radio became louder as the door to his cabin opened. A brown Indian face looked in at him.

"Hey, Skipper, chow's ready below." The face vanished.

Slowly he got out of his bunk and onto the deck. He stood in front of the mirror. Cautiously he pressed his fingers against his eyelids and morbidly enjoyed the pain it gave him. He noticed his eyes were bloodshot and his face was grimy. He scowled at himself in the mirror. From the wheelhouse the sound of Negro music thudded painfully in his ears.

"Turn that damn thing off!" he shouted.

"O.K., Skipper," his second mate's voice answered. The music faded away and he began to dress. The second mate came into the cabin. "Quite a party, wasn't it, Mr Evans?"

Evans grunted. "Some party. What time is it?"

The mate looked at his watch. "Six-twenty."

Evans closed his eyes and began to count to himself: one, two—he had had four hours and thirty minutes of

1

sleep. That was too little sleep. The mate was watching him. "You don't look so good," he said finally.

"I know it." He picked up his tie. "Anything new? Weather look all right?"

The mate sat down on the bunk and ran his hands through his hair. It was an irritating habit. His hair was long and the color of mouldering straw; when he relaxed he fingered it. On board a ship one noticed such things.

"Weather looks fine. A little wind from the south but not enough to hurt. We scraped some paint off the bow last night. I guess we were too close to that piling." He pushed back his hair and left it alone. Evans was glad of that.

"We'll have to paint the whole ship this month anyway." Evans buttoned the pockets of his olive-drab shirt. High-ranking officers were apt to criticize, even in the Aleutians. He pinned the Warrant Officer insignia on his collar. His hands shook.

Bervick watched him. "You really had some party, I guess."

"That's right. Joe's going back to the States on rotation. We were celebrating. It was some party all right." Evans rubbed his eyes. "Have you had chow yet, Bervick?"

The mate, Bervick, nodded. "I had it with the cooks. I've been around since five." He stood up. He was shorter than Evans and Evans was not tall. Bervick was lightly built; he had large gray Norwegian eyes, and there were many fine lines about his eyes. He was an old seaman at thirty.

"I think I'll go below now," said Evans. He stepped out of his cabin and into the wheelhouse, glancing automatically at the barometer. The needle pointed between Fair and Change; this was usual. He went below. At the end of the companionway, the doors to the engine room were open and the generator was going. The twin Diesel engines were silent. He went into the galley.

John Smith, the Indian cook, was kneading dough. He was a bad cook from southeastern Alaska. Cooks of any kind were scarce, though, and Evans was glad to have even this bad one.

"What's new?" asked Evans, preparing to listen to Smitty's many troubles.

"The new cook." Smitty pointed to a fat man in a white apron gathering dishes in the dining salon.

"What's wrong now?"

"I ask him to wash dishes last night. It was his turn, but he won't do nothing like that. So I tell him what I think. I tell him off good, but he no listen. I seen everything now. . . ." Smitty's black eyes glittered as he talked. Evans stopped him.

"O.K. I'll talk to him." He went into the dining salon. Here two tables ran parallel to the bulkheads. One table was for the crew; the other for the ship's officers and the engineers. The crew's table was empty; only the Chief Engineer, Duval, sat at the other table.

"Morning, Skipper," he said. He was an older man. His hair was gray and black in streaks. It was clipped very short. His nose was long and hooked and his mouth was wide but not pleasant. Duval was a New Orleans Frenchman.

"Good morning, Chief. Looks like everybody's up early today."

"Yeah, I guess they are at that." The Chief cleared his throat. He waited for a comment. There was none. Then he remarked casually, "I guess it's because they all heard we was going to Arunga. I guess that's just a rumor." He looked at his fork. Evans could see that he was anxious to know if they were leaving. The Chief would never ask a direct question, though.

The fat cook put a plate of eggs in front of Evans and poured him some black coffee. The cook's hand was unsteady and the coffee spilled on the table. The cook ignored the puddle of coffee, and went back into the galley.

Evans watched the brown liquid drip slowly off onto the deck. Dreamily he made patterns with his forefinger. He thought of Arunga island. Finally he said, "I wonder where they pick up rumors like that?"

"Just about anywhere," said the Chief. "They probably figured we was going there because that's our port's headquarters and the General's Adjutant is here and they say he's breaking his back to get back fast and that there aren't no planes flying out for a week. We're the only ship in the harbor that could take him to Arunga."

"That sounds pretty interesting," said Evans and he began to eat. Duval scowled and pushed back his chair from the table. He stood up and stretched himself. "Arunga's a nice trip anyway." He waited for a remark. Again there was none. "Think I'll go look at the engines."

Evans smiled as he left. Duval did not think highly of him. Evans was easily half the Chief Engineer's age and that meant trouble. The Chief thought that age was a substitute for both brains and experience; Evans could not like that idea. He knew, however, that he would eventually have to tell the Chief that they were leaving for Arunga.

Evans ate quickly. He noticed that the first mate's place was untouched. He would have to speak to him again about getting up earlier.

Breakfast over, he left the salon by the after door. He stood on the stern and breathed deeply. The sky was gray. A filmy haze hung over the harbor and there was no wind. The water of the harbor was like a dark glass. Overhead the sea gulls darted about, looking for scraps on the water. A quiet day for winter in these islands.

Evans climbed over the starboard side and stepped down on the dock. There were two large warehouses on the dock. They were military and impermanent. Several power barges were moored near his ship and he would have to let his bow swing far out when they left; mechanically, he figured time and distance.

Longshoremen in soiled blue coveralls were loading the barges, and the various crews, civilians and soldiers mixed, were preparing to cast off for their day's work in the harbor.

A large wooden-faced Indian skipper shouted at Evans from the wheelhouse of one of the barges. Evans shouted back a jovial curse; then he turned and walked across the dock to the shore.

Andrefski Bay was the main harbor for this Aleutian island. The bay was well protected, and, though not large, there were no reefs or shallow places in the main part of the harbor. No trees grew on the island. The only vegetation was a coarse brown turf which furred the low hills that edged the bay. Beyond these low hills were high, sharp and pyramidal mountains, blotched with snow.

Evans looked at the mountains but did not see them. He had seen them many times before and they were of no interest to him now. He never noticed them. He thought of the trip to Arunga. A good trip to make, a long one, three days, that was the best thing about going. He had found that when they were too much in port everyone got a little bored and irritable. A change would be good now.

Someone called his name. He looked behind him. The second mate, Bervick, was hurrying toward him.

"Going over to the office, Skipper?" he asked, when he had caught up.

"That's right. Going to pick up our orders."

"Arunga?"

"Yes." They walked on together.

The second mate was not wearing his Technical Sergeant's stripes. Evans hoped the Adjutant would not mind. One could never tell about these Headquarters people. He would warn Bervick later.

They walked slowly along the black volcanic ash roadway. At various intervals there were wooden huts and warehouses. Between many of the buildings equipment was piled, waiting to be shipped out.

"It's been almost a year since we was to Arunga," remarked Bervick.

"That's right."

"Have we got some new charts?"

"We got them last fall, remember?"

"I guess I forgot." A large truck went by them and they stood in the shallow gutter until it had passed.

"You seen the sheep woman lately?" asked Evans.

The sheep woman was the only woman on the island. She was a Canadian who helped run the sheep ranch in the interior. She had been on the island for several years, and, though middle-aged, stout, and reasonably virtuous, the rumors about her were damning. It was said that she charged fifty dollars for her services and everyone thought that that was too much.

Bervick shook his head. "I don't know how she's doing. O.K., I suppose. I'm saving up for when we hit the Big Harbor next. I don't want nothing to do with her."

Evans was interested. "Who've you got in mind at Big Harbor?"

"Olga."

"I thought she was the Chief's property."

Bervick shrugged. "That's what he says. She's a good girl."

"I suppose so."

"I like her. The Chief's just blowing."

"None of them are worth much trouble."

A light rain began to fall. The office was still half a mile ahead of them. All the buildings of the port were, for the sake of protection, far apart.

"Damn it," muttered Evans, as the rain splattered in his face. A truck came up behind them. It stopped and they climbed into the back. Evans told the driver where they were going, then he turned to Bervick. "You better pick up the weather forecast today."

"I will. I think it'll be pretty good."

"Hard to say. This is funny weather."

The truck let them off at the Army Transport Service Office. The office was housed in a long, one-storied, gray building.

The outer room was large, and here four or five enlisted men were doing clerical work beneath fluorescent lights. The walls were decorated with posters warning against poison gas, faulty camouflage, and venereal disease.

One of the clerks spoke to Evans. "The Captain's waiting for you," he said.

"I think I'll go check with Weather," said Bervick. "I'll see you back to the boat."

"Fine." Evans walked down a corridor to the Captain's office.

A desk and three neat uncomfortable chairs furnished the room. On the walls were pictures of the

President, several Generals, and several nudes. The nudes usually came down during inspections.

The Captain was sitting hunched over his desk. He was a heavy man with large features. He was smoking a pipe and talking at the same time to a Major who sat in one of the three uncomfortable chairs. They looked up as Evans entered.

"Hello there, Skipper," said the Captain and he took his pipe out of his mouth. "I want you to meet an old friend of mine, Major Barkison."

The Major stood up and shook hands with Evans. "Glad to know you, Mister . . ."

"Evans."

"Mister Evans. It looks as if you'll be pressed into service."

"Yes it does . . . sir." He added the "sir" just in case.

"I hope the trip will be a calm one," remarked the Major with a smile.

"It should be." Evans relaxed. The Major seemed to be human.

Major Barkison was a West Pointer and quietly proud of the fact. Though not much over thirty he was already bald. He had a Roman nose, pale blue eyes, and a firm but small chin. He looked like the Duke of Wellington. Knowing this, he hoped that someone might someday mention the resemblance; no one ever did, though.

"Sit down here, Evans," said the Captain, pointing to one of the chairs. The Major and Evans both sat down. "We're sending you out on a little trip to Arunga. Out west where the deer and submarines play." He laughed heartily at his joke. Evans also laughed. The Major did not.

The Major said, "How long will the trip take you?"

"That's hard to say." Evans figured for a moment in his head. "Seventy hours is about average. We can't tell until we know the weather."

Barkison nodded and said nothing.

The Captain blew a smoke ring and watched it float ceilingward, his little eyes almost shut. "The weather reports are liable to be pretty lousy," he said at last.

Barkison nodded again. "Yes, that's right. That's why I can't fly out of here for at least a week. Everything's grounded. That's why I can't get out of here. It is imperative that I get back to Headquarters."

"The war would stop if you didn't get back, wouldn't it, Major?" The Captain said this jovially but Evans thought there was malice in what he said.

"What do you mean, Captain?" said the Major stiffly.

"Nothing at all, sir. I was just joking. A bad habit of ours here." Evans smiled to himself. He knew that the Captain did not like regular army men. The Captain had been in the grain business and he was proud that he made more money than the men in the regular army. They did not understand business and the Captain did. This made a difference. The Major frowned.

"I have to get my reports in, you know. You understand that, of course. You know I would never have a boat sent out in weather like this unless it were important. This weather precludes air travel," he added somewhat pompously, enjoying the word "preclude." It had an official sound.

"Certainly, Major." The Captain turned to Evans. "From what I gather the trip shouldn't be too bad, a little rough perhaps, but then it usually is. You had better put into the Big Harbor tomorrow and get a weather briefing there. I got some cargo for them, too. I told the boys to load you up today." He paused to chew on his pipe. "By the way," he said in a different voice, "how do you feel after our little party last night?"

Evans grimaced. "Not very good. The stuff tasted like raisin jack."

"You should know." The Captain laughed loudly and winked. Barkison looked pained. He cleared his throat.

"I guess you people have a hard time getting liquor up here." He tried to sound like one of the boys and failed.

"We manage." The Captain chuckled.

The door opened. A young and pink-faced Lieutenant looked doubtfully about the room until he saw the Major.

"Come in, Lieutenant," said the Major.

"Lieutenant Hodges, this is Mr Evans." The two shook hands and sat down. The young Lieutenant was very solemn.

"Is there anything new on our leaving, sir?" he asked.

"Yes," said Barkison. "Weather permitting, we'll leave tomorrow morning. We should be back . . . how long did you say?"

"Maybe three days, maybe less," Evans answered.

"Isn't that awfully long, sir? I mean we have to be back day after tomorrow."

The Major shrugged. "Nothing we can do about it. There are no planes going out for an indefinite period."

"Well," the Captain stood up and Evans did the same, "you had better check on the weather and take water and do whatever else you have to do. You'll definitely leave tomorrow morning and you'll stop off at the Big Harbor. See you later today." He turned to the Major. "If you'd like to move aboard tonight. . . ."

"Oh no, never mind. We'll move on tomorrow."

"O.K., be seeing you, Evans."

Evans muttered that he had been pleased to meet them and left the room. As he walked down the corridor he wondered if Bervick would be able to understand the weather chart. He decided not.

Outside, the rain had stopped. The wind was cooler and more brisk. Evans walked toward a half-barrel-shaped hut: the weather office. Ravens glided heavily around him, their black feathers glistening bluely in the pale light. High above him he could make out an eagle flying northward.

Inside the weather office a Master Sergeant was handling the maps and charts. The weather officer had not come in yet.

"Hello, Mr Evans."

"Hello, has Bervick been here?"

"Yes, he just now left. I think he's gone to get some paint over to Supply."

"I see. What's the deal on the weather?"

The Sergeant shuffled his papers. "It's hard to say. If the wind shifts around to the north, and it looks like it will, you'll be fine."

"Is there much wind outside the harbor?"

"There's some."

"Much wind? Thirty mile an hour? Is it more?"

"Damned if I can tell. You're leaving tomorrow, aren't you?"

"That's right."

"Well, I'll check with the Navy boys and get in touch with you later. This isn't a good month for traveling the Chain."

"I know. Is that the weather chart you got there?"

"Yes." The Sergeant pushed the chart at him. Evans pretended to study it. Actually he knew very little about reading these charts. He knew from practical experience, though, that they were often wrong.

"It'll probably be rough, Mr Evans."

"That's nothing new. You say Bervick's at Supply?"

"I think so."

"O.K., and thanks a lot. I'll see you when you have some more dope." Evans went out. He stood for a while watching the power barges, blunt-nosed and slab-like, move back and forth across the harbor. There were rumors that the port of Andrefski was to be closed soon and only the inland air base would be kept going. Many men had already been moved out, only a few hundred were left now. On the rocky, moonstone and agate littered beach, lumber was piled, waiting to be loaded on the Liberty ship, edged grayly against the main dock. This ship was the largest in the harbor and it made the other boats look like toys in a bathtub.

A jeep, with an awkward plywood body tacked onto it, rode by and splashed him with mud from the side of the road. Evans swore at the driver. Then he walked along the road, keeping close to the pebbled embankment. There was quite a lot of traffic at this time of day.

The Supply warehouse was large and gloomy and empty-looking. He walked around to the side of the building and went inside. He could hear Bervick's voice. "Come on, you can give us six gallons. Christ, you have the stuff piled up all around."

Another voice answered, "Sorry, three's all you get."

"Why that's. . . ." Evans walked up to them. Bervick was holding three gallon cans of paint.

Evans grinned, "That'll do us fine, Bervick. Are you through here?"

"I guess so."

"Well, let's get on back to the ship." Bervick picked up two of the cans and Evans took the other.

A thin drizzle was beginning to cloud the air.

"Nice day," said Bervick.

"Yes, nice day. All days are nice here. We go to the Big Harbor tomorrow."

"And from there to Arunga?"

"That's right. We got some rank to carry."

"Who? I heard the Chaplain might come."

"That's a new one. I hadn't heard about him. We've got a Major who is the Adjutant at Arunga, and a Lieutenant."

"Any cargo?"

"Some for the Big Harbor. That's all."

They walked along the road, their feet grinding the wet cinder-like surface. Sea gulls circled high above them, a sign of bad weather according to the Indians. Among the sharp rocks the ravens croaked drearily. Silently they walked back to the ship.

Two of the men were hosing down the deck. The sea water from their hoses made a drumming sound as it shot across the decks.

Evans was surprised. "The first time they've ever done this without being told."

Bervick laughed, "The crew knew we were going before you did."

"They usually do."

They climbed aboard. Bervick went aft with the paint. Evans opened the door to the dining salon and stepped inside.

The Chief, sitting on one of the tables, was smoking a cigar. Down the companionway, Evans could see the two assistant engineers working on the auxiliary.

"What's new, Skipper?" asked Duval.

"Hello, Chief. Your boys pretty busy?"

"Yeah, getting ready for the big trip. Lucky we took fuel last week."

"It was."

"When we leaving?" The Chief asked one of his few direct questions.

"Tomorrow morning."

"Straight to Arunga, I suppose."

"No, we're going to the Big Harbor first. We go on from there."

"I guess I'll be able to see Olga then." The Chief grinned.

Evans looked at him. "What about Bervick?"

"What about him?" The Chief was not interested and they said nothing for a few moments. Then he said, "I hear the Chaplain'll be with us."

"So I've heard. I guess the Captain will tell me about it later."

"Probably. I got to get to work." The Chief slid off the table and walked toward the engine room. Evans could hear the sound of his voice as he talked with his assistants. Evans knew he was telling them that they were going west to Arunga as he had said they would. Evans walked into the galley. The cook, John Smith, was scrubbing pans. He was alone in the galley.

"How's it going, Smitty? Where's your helper?"

Smitty put down the kettle he was scrubbing. "Gone," he said with suppressed drama. "I seen everything now. What does this guy do? Does this guy help in here? No. He go down and lay on his fat butt. I'm going to get off this boat. I seen everything. He won't work, won't do nothing. . . ."

"I'll talk to him, Smitty." That was always a good promise to make. Smitty would be mad at something else the next day anyway. "By the way," he added, "have you got enough rations to get us to Arunga? We're going to have three passengers."

Smitty gasped. His lean ugly brown face was contorted with grief. "I seen *everything* now." He spoke softly as if he were praying. "I got no bread. I got no meat. I got no nothing now. How," his voice rose to a wail, "how am I going to feed the crew? I make no bread on the water. They eat out of cans, that's all."

"Well, you work it out and get what you need. We'll leave tomorrow at eight."

Smitty muttered to himself. Evans went up to the wheelhouse.

Bervick was standing over the chart table: a chart of all the islands in the Aleutian Chain before him. He was squinting thoughtfully and carefully measuring out a course.

"Think you can get us there?" asked Evans.

"What? Oh sure, I was just checking the old course. Last time we ran too close to shore off Kulak."

"I remember. We'll work out a course over at the Big Harbor." The salt spray from the hoses splattered the wheelhouse windows. "That reminds me, you better get some water. We're pretty low."

"O.K." Bervick put the chart in a drawer under the table and left the wheelhouse.

Evans looked out the window. He could think of nothing very important to be done before they sailed. They had fuel. Smitty would get rations. The charts were up to date. He rubbed his face to see if he needed a shave. He did.

Evans went into his cabin and turned on the water in his basin. He noticed that his eyes looked a little better, though they still hurt him. He sighed and tried to look at his profile in the glass. This he knew would exercise his eyes, also in the back of his mind he wondered if he might not be able to see his profile. He had seen it once in a tailor's three-way mirror. He had been greatly interested, and he hoped vaguely that he might see it again sometime. Strange things like that obsessed people who had been to sea for a long time.

Someone turned on the radio. A deep sterile radio voice staccatoed in the air for a moment and was gone. The air was filled with static, and then the voice came back again. Evans could not make out what the voice was saying but he could guess from the tone that our "forces were smashing ahead on all fronts": the usual thing. He was bored by the war.

Methodically he shaved himself. He wondered who had turned on the radio. Probably Martin, his first mate.

A light wisp of fog came into the room through the

half-open window; quickly Evans shut it. He shivered. The cold was penetrating.

"I'm cold as gold is old," he muttered to himself. It was a jingle that went occasionally through his mind. For several years he had known it. Queer phrases and jingles often came to him when he had been too much alone. Sometimes they worried him. Evans often wondered if he might not be a little crazy. They say, though, that when you are crazy you never know it, he thought. There was consolation in that and he murmured again to himself, "I'm cold as gold is old." Then he finished shaving.

He looked much older than twenty-five, he noticed, looking at himself intently in the mirror. When he was eighteen he had worked alone in a lighthouse. He used often to look at himself in the mirror then. He felt less alone when he did that and the habit had stayed with him. He yawned and turned away from the mirror. Neatly he put his shaving equipment away, then he sat down at his desk and looked at the papers on it. Most of the papers were memorandums from the Headquarters. He pushed them to one side.

In his desk drawer was a quart of bourbon. He wondered if he should take a swallow, a small one, enough to take away the ache behind his eyes. Evans reached for the drawer. Before he could open it, Martin walked into the cabin. Martin never knocked.

"Good morning," said Evans and he tried to sound sarcastic.

"Hail to the Chief," said Martin, eying Evans' hand on the liquor drawer. "Starting in early, aren't you?"

"What do you mean? Oh, this," Evans withdrew his hand quickly. "I was just looking for something."

"So I see." The first mate smiled, showing all his teeth. He was a year younger than Evans, but looked even younger than he was. He had a carefully studied collegiate manner though he had never been to a college. John Martin had been one of the numerous unpromising young actors in a New England stock company. He was dark and nearly handsome. His voice was deep, interesting and mocking. He knew nothing about being a mate.

"Did you just get up?" Evans asked, knowing that he had.

"Why yes—the party, you know. I felt I should sleep. The ravell'd sleave, you know." He spoke with a pseudo-British accent which he knew irritated Evans.

"Well, go get on down below and make sure they take water," Evans snapped.

"Right you are, sir."

"Can the funny stuff. We're going to the Big Harbor tomorrow."

"Any passengers?"

"Yes, the Adjutant at Arunga, a Lieutenant and the Chaplain."

"That sounds gay. When're we going to haul another group of USO girls?" Martin winked in what he would have called a roguish manner. Evans had once become too interested in a USO girl on tour.

Evans murmured, "Not for a while." He turned away and played with the papers on his desk. He tried to think of something for Martin to do. "You might," he finally said, "go see the Chaplain and find out when he's coming aboard. Also, you'd better get hold of a copy of the special orders with his name on them. The Captain forgot to tell me he was going."

"Fine." Martin started to go. "By the way," he said, and Evans knew and dreaded what he was going to say, "how do you feel after the party last night? You don't look so good."

"I feel awful. Now go get to work."

Martin left and Evans rested his head on his arm. He felt tired. The ship was unusually still. Far away he could hear the rasping croak of a raven. He opened the desk drawer.

ii

John Martin walked into the galley.

"What's on your mind, Smitty?" he asked. Martin was always polite with the men and Evans was not. The men liked Martin better and that was the main reason why Evans did not like him, or so Martin thought.

"Nothing on my mind. You want to eat something?"

"No thanks. I'll just take a little of this." He poured himself some pineapple juice from a large can. Smitty watched him drink it.

"What's on for chow tonight?"

The Indian's eyes gleamed. "Vienna sausage and that's all I got. I have to go get rations for a whole week now. I haven't got no time to make bread or nothing. That guy," he pointed upward, "he tell me just today to get this stuff."

"Well, that's O.K., Smitty," Martin murmured soothingly, as he left, "it'll be all right."

On deck he found two of the crew coiling the long black water hose.

"Pretty empty, wasn't she?"

One of them nodded. He was a heavy blond fellow, a professional seaman. "Are we going out west?" he asked.

"That's right. Leaving tomorrow."

"That's what Bervick said. We didn't know what he was bulling or not. Weather don't look bad."

Martin looked at the pale sky. "You can't ever tell," he said.

"No, you can't." They went on coiling the hose.

Martin walked across the dock. He watched lumber being loaded onto the Liberty ship by sailors with heavy fantastic beards. The port was slowly closing down and he, for one, was not sorry. For a year now he had been at Andrefski as a first mate. He had fought constantly with Evans and he had known all the time that Evans was right: that he was no seaman. Martin had drifted into boat work in the army. After two years he had been made a Warrant Officer and assigned to this Freight-Passenger ship. The whole thing was unreal to him, the Bering Sea, these boats, the desolate stone islands. He wished he were in New England and the thought that he would be at least another year in these islands was maddening.

Thinking of these things, he walked to the warehouse where the mail was delivered. A door in the warehouse opened and Bervick came out. He carried a bundle of letters in his hand. "Hello, Johnny," he said. "You up so soon?"

Martin smiled. There was no formality between them. Living together in the same small stateroom they understood each other well. "I thought a run in the fog would be just what I needed. Got something for me?"

Bervick thumbed through the bundle and handed Martin a letter. "How does it smell?" he asked.

Martin inhaled the perfume that had been sprinkled on the envelope. "Like magnolias," he said.

Bervick sniffed. "Smells like a Ketchikan whore to me."

"Careful," said Martin, "speak softly when you speak of love. Which reminds me, when are they going to load cargo?"

"Right after lunch, I suppose. That's if the longshoremen can get together long enough to do some work."

"Then you'd better move the boom over."

"O.K." Bervick walked away.

Martin stepped inside the warehouse. Standing close to the door—there was almost no light in the building —he read the perfumed letter. She thought a lot about him. She wondered how he was. She did not go out much. She wished he were back. She did not go out much, she repeated that. She wondered if he remembered when . . . Martin folded the letter and put it in his pocket. Her letters were always the same but she was a nice girl and he would probably marry her and be bored. He felt sorry for himself. He looked at the bleak sky and saw that it suited his mood.

A blast of damp air came through the door and he buttoned his parka at the throat. Then, remembering his errand with the Chaplain, he walked out into the gray light.

A mile away on a slight mound was the post chapel. It was like all other army chapels: box-shaped, with a short square tower and spire. The building was brown and looked dingy from camouflage. He walked toward it.

The wind blew at his back. The wind was rising and

there were whitecaps in the bay. Gulls flew worriedly in the bedrizzled air.

A jeep went by him on the road. It stopped and he climbed in. The Captain was sitting at the wheel, his pipe firmly between his teeth.

"How's the boat business, Martin?" he asked cheerfully.

"Fine as ever."

"Good." He started the jeep. "Where are you headed?"

"Over to see the Chaplain. I hear he's coming with us."

"Damn! I knew I forgot to tell Evans something. The Chaplain's going with you people. They're having a meeting at Arunga and he's already on orders. Does Evans know?"

"Yes, he heard about it."

"Grapevine," the Captain muttered. "I'm going as far as the Post Exchange. You want out there?"

"That'll be fine."

The Captain drove deliberately and in silence over the road. After a few minutes he stopped in front of a long low building and they both got out. They walked into the Post Exchange.

"You getting on all right with Evans?" the Captain asked.

"Sure, we're coming along fine," Martin said, trying to sound sincere and succeeding.

"That's the way things should be. I'm glad to hear it."

The Post Exchange was not yet crowded. A long counter ran the length of the building and behind the counter there were shelves of candy, stationery, toilet articles, magazines. . . . At one end of the building was a barber's chair and a soldier barber, and at the other end was a Coca-Cola machine. Everything was neatly arranged beneath hard bare electric lights.

Martin bought a lurid Love magazine. Nothing else caught his eye and he left.

He was out of breath when he reached the top of the mound where the chapel was. A few enlisted men were wandering about near by, getting up enough nerve to go in and see the Chaplain and ask for help. This Chaplain had a reputation for being able to get things done for the men. The religious aura, however, was unmanning to most of them.

The inside of the chapel was quiet and dim and warm. There was little ornament here, only an altar and plain, large-windowed walls without color or design. In a small office to the right of the door, Martin found O'Mahoney, the Chaplain.

He was a short squat Irishman with a red-veined nose, plump cheeks and nearsighted blue eyes. His hair was thick and dark and looked like a neat wig. His manner was awkward and friendly. He had been a monk in a Maryland monastery, and now, in the army, he acted as if he were playing a part in a bad dream, which perhaps he was.

"Hello, Father," said Martin respectfully.

"How do you do. . . ." O'Mahoney paused with embarrassment. Martin was not a churchgoer and he did not recognize him.

"John Martin, sir," he said quickly. "I'm the first mate on the boat that's taking you to Arunga."

O'Mahoney smiled. "Do sit down, Mr Martin," he invited. Martin arranged himself with a sigh in a large armchair. He was tired from his walk. For a moment he breathed the musty leather smell which all churches seemed to have. O'Mahoney offered him a cigarette. He refused and said that he did not smoke.

"A good habit not to have," said the Chaplain in his light Irish voice. There was a pause.

"I wanted to know," began Martin in a loud voice which he quickly lowered. He was always conscious of wrong tones. A loud voice was wrong in a church. "I was wondering," he said softly, "when you were planning to move aboard, tonight or in the morning."

"Tomorrow, if that's convenient."

"It will be." Martin smiled. "You'll be ready for bad weather, won't you?"

"Bad weather? Is that the report?"

"Well, yes, but it's also a joke of ours that whenever we haul a Chaplain we have bad weather."

O'Mahoney chuckled uneasily. "Well, that's the way those things go, I suppose."

"Yes, it's probably just an invitation for you to walk on the water."

"What? Oh, yes." O'Mahoney was not quite sure if this was blasphemy or not. He decided it was not. "Are you Catholic, Mr Martin?" he asked. He usually asked that question.

Martin shook his head. "I'm not much of anything," he said. He could see that the Chaplain was tempted to inquire further. He did not, though. Instead he changed the subject.

"The Captain at the Transport Office did tell me that the weather might be unreliable at this time of year."

"That's right, but it shouldn't be bad." Martin spoke as if the sea and the weather had no secrets from him. Often he marveled at how professional he sounded.

"I'm certainly glad to hear that. I suffer terribly from *mal de mer*." He spoke the French self-consciously and Martin wondered if he was going to translate it or not. He decided to save him the trouble.

"I'm sure you won't be sick, Father." Martin got to his feet. "If you want to send any stuff down tonight, we'll stow it for you."

"Thank you, but I'll bring my gear down with me in the morning."

Martin turned to go, then he remembered the orders he had come to get. "Do you think I could have an extra copy of your orders? We have to have one, you know."

"Certainly." O'Mahoney handed him a paper from his desk.

"Thank you. See you tomorrow."

"Aren't you going to the Captain's party tonight, Mr Martin? He's giving one in his quarters for the Major."

"Why, yes, I suppose I will."

"See you then." The Chaplain walked with him to the door.

iii

Bervick and Duval were arguing again. Supper had been finished and Evans had gone to the wheelhouse. Martin sat quietly in a corner while the Chief and Bervick insulted each other. Their arguments were thought very funny by the rest of the crew. No one took them seriously except Martin, and he was not sure if they were serious or not.

Olga, a Norwegian girl at the Big Harbor, was the cause of their trouble. The year before she had come to work in a restaurant. Because she had let Bervick sleep with her for nothing, he had decided that it must be love and he had almost decided to marry her. Then one day he discovered that she was also seeing Duval and accepting his money and a great many other people's money, too. He had asked her to stop but she was a thrifty girl, supporting her mother in Canada. She had told him that it was none of his business. Duval had laughed at him because of this and he had come to hate Duval and feel that it was his fault that Olga had changed.

Somewhat drowsily Martin listened to them talk. This time they were arguing whether the knife should be set on the table edge of blade toward the plate or away from it. Duval claimed the edge should be away from the plate and Bervick claimed it was toward the plate.

"I don't suppose you'd know where it went anyway," said Duval bitingly. "You probably always ate with your hands."

This was a hard blow and Bervick countered, "I don't guess you ever used anything but a knife to eat with. I've seen *cajuns* like you before."

Duval was proud of his pure French ancestry. He came from a long-settled New Orleans family and he was sensitive about being thought a *cajun*.

"*Cajun,* hell," he said, trying not to sound irritated. "You wouldn't know one if you saw one."

"I guess I'm talking to one."

This was too much. The Chief Engineer remembered

his rank. He stood up. "That's enough, Sergeant," he said with dignity.

Bervick stood up also. Martin could see he was pleased. It was always a victory when the Chief fell back on his rank. "Yes, Warrant Officer Junior Grade Duval," he said.

"Better not get so fresh, Sergeant." The Chief turned to Martin and said, "Just a little squabble." Bervick left the salon, laughing. "Fresh bastard," muttered the Chief.

"Oh, he's all right," said Martin smoothly. "Just a little hot-tempered at times."

"Maybe that's it." Duval sat down on the bench beside Martin. They looked out the window at the pale gray of evening. The day was over and the wind had died down.

"Probably be a strong southwest wind tomorrow," remarked Duval.

"Can't tell, really."

"Thank God we've only a few passengers. Every time it's rough we have at least forty."

"That's the way it goes."

At the other table five deckhands were playing Hearts. Martin watched them. His thoughts drifted and he saw stages and heard speeches and listened to the sea. The sea was becoming a part of himself, and whenever he relaxed, his mind seemed to be caught up in the restless tempo of the water and he would become uneasy: at sea he was always uneasy. He yawned abruptly and cleared his mind.

Evans came into the salon. "Say, Mate," he said, "the Captain's giving a party over at his quarters. You and the Chief want to come?"

Martin nodded. "I always like free beer."

"So do I." The Chief got to his feet. "I hope he's got some bourbon. I haven't had any good stuff for quite a while. It gets used up so fast because I always share it." The Chief knew of Evans' liquor and he also knew that Evans never shared it. Evans looked away.

"We'd better get started then. The dispatcher's waiting outside. He's going to take us over in his jeep."

The Captain's quarters consisted of two huts knocked together. Normally three officers lived there, but at the moment he was alone and had the whole place to himself.

Several men were already in the room when they entered. The Captain was fixing drinks behind a bar made out of a packing case. He grunted at them, his pipe moving slightly as he greeted them.

Evans and Duval were jovial in their greetings. Martin merely smiled. The Chief was on particularly good terms with the Captain. They were of the same age and had had many parties together.

"How does it go, Old Chief?" inquired the Captain, speaking out of the side of his mouth.

"Great. We keep the army on the waves."

"That's something. What'll it be, gentlemen?" While the others told what they wanted, Martin looked about him. He had not been in the Captain's quarters for a long time. He never liked to seem too close to higher ranking officers. He was always afraid someone would think he wanted something.

The walls were decorated with large paintings of nudes. They had been done for the Captain by a soldier. A lamp, several chairs, and a bookcase with a few books and a great many rocks in it furnished this end of the room.

A Major and a Lieutenant were standing before one of the paintings. Martin, who did not recognize them, decided that they must be the passengers for Arunga. In one corner beside a radio the Chaplain sat, a pale bourbon and water beside him. He was turning the dial of the radio. Three officers from the Harbor Craft Detachment made up the rest of the party.

"What'll it be, Martin?" asked the Captain.

"Beer, if you have it."

"Beer! O.K., suit yourself. I'm always glad to save the real stuff." He handed Martin a bottle of beer.

Loud music startled them. The Chaplain looked about him apologetically and quickly lowered the volume. "Finally got some music," he announced. "The static isn't so bad tonight."

The Major agreed, "Yes, the static's not bad at all tonight."

The Lieutenant remarked that the static had been bad the night before.

That, thought Martin, takes care of the static. He often wondered why people spoke so inanely.

"These are very interesting works of . . . of art, you have here," remarked the Major somewhat archly. Martin could see that he was trying to be a good fellow.

"Like them?" The Captain came out from behind the bar. "Had a soldier do them for me. Very talented fellow he was, too. Quite lifelike, aren't they?" He winked at the young Lieutenant, who blushed and looked away. Martin chuckled and noticed that the Major was smiling, too.

The Major said, "Lieutenant Hodges doesn't care for modern art."

The Captain laughed, "Oh, to be young! Wouldn't it be nice, Major, if we were young again."

The Major winced slightly. He was not old and did not like to be thought old, but because he was bald and his face was lined, people took him to be older than he was. He did not like that.

"Youth is very important," he murmured, paying no attention to what he was saying.

"Most important for the future," agreed the Chaplain.

Martin was bored by this. He took his beer and sat down in an easy chair. He drank the beer slowly. It was green and tasted bitter. He watched Evans and Duval draw near to the Major. Both were good politicians.

"It looks as if the war will be over soon," remarked Evans, a half-question in his voice.

"Yes," said the Major. He always said "yes" first, even when he meant "no."

"Yes, it should be over soon, but of course we have no effective way of gauging the enemy's rate of attrition. The attrition rate is important. Attrition can decide wars." Martin wondered if he would repeat this last: it sounded like a maxim. He did not. He continued. "There are only a few good strategists in the enemy's army. They could be named on the fingers of one hand. Most of them know nothing but frontal attacks."

"I guess bombings are messing them up," suggested Evans.

"Wars," said the Major, "cannot be won by aviation. No matter what the Air Corps says." He sounded bitter. Martin wondered if the Major might not be jealous of the quick promotions in the Air Corps.

"I guess that's right," Evans agreed.

Everyone began to talk at once. Evans and the Major discussed the latest movies. The Chief, who was Catholic, discussed moral issues with the Chaplain. One always seemed to discuss such things with Chaplains. The Captain talked about women and the Lieutenant listened to him gravely.

Cigarette smoke was becoming thick in the room. Blue veils of it floated upward from each smoker. Martin's eyes watered. He finished his beer. The radio played on. Music of every sort swelled in the room. The room was too hot. The oil-stove in the center was giving off heavy waves of heat. Martin felt a little drowsy. He wondered if they would notice it if he shut his eyes for a moment.

Lieutenant Hodges was standing beside his chair, when he opened his eyes again.

"Must have been asleep," Martin mumbled. His eyes felt heavy. He looked around and saw that the others obviously had not noticed he had gone to sleep. They were talking and singing and drinking. There was a strong barroom odor in the hut. The Chaplain, he noticed, had gone.

"Sorry to bother you," said the Lieutenant. "I didn't mean to wake you."

"That's all right. I don't know what happened to me. I was just tired, I guess. I've had a pretty hard day," he lied.

"You're on the boat that's taking us west, aren't you?"

"Yes. I'm the mate. Martin's the name."

"My name is Hodges. I'm the Major's assistant." They shook hands in the self-conscious manner of people who have already met.

There was not much to say. They stood there watching the others move about. Almost everyone was drunk.

Martin got slowly to his feet. "What time you got?" he asked.

Hodges looked at his watch carefully. "Eleven fifty-seven."

"That's pretty late for me to be up. I guess I better get a move on. See you in the morning."

"Sure thing. Good night."

Martin went over to the corner where Evans, the Major, and the Captain were singing.

"I think we'd better head back," he said, catching Evans between songs. Evans shook his head. He was drunk.

"Hell no," he said. "You go back if you want to. You go back."

Martin shrugged and turned away. The Chief was in a crap game with an Indian skipper.

"Can't leave now," the Chief said, his eyes on the dice.

Martin picked up his parka and put it on.

"I think I'll walk back," he announced. Hodges was the only one who heard and he nodded as Martin turned to go.

The Major was talking of strategy when he left.

"Wellington, of course, was the perfect general. Wellington understood attrition. Attrition. . . ." The Major talked on.

Outside Martin breathed the deep night air gratefully. It was good after the heat and smoke. There were no stars out yet and that was not good. With a shiver he turned and walked quickly toward the docks.

Chapter Two

i

"It's seven o'clock, Mr Evans." The man on watch looked into his room.

"O.K., be right down," Evans mumbled. The door was slammed shut and he opened his eyes. It was another morning. His bed was warm and the room, lit grayly by the morning sun, was cold. He closed his eyes and imagined that he was out of bed and already dressed. He imagined this clearly; so clearly that he began to fall asleep again. The sound of dishes being dropped startled him awake. He sat up in bed and put on his shirt. Then, quickly, so as not to feel the cold, he sprang out of bed and finished dressing. He was brushing his teeth when Bervick came in the room.

"Morning, Skipper, nice party? I heard you come in this morning." Evans wondered why his second mate always seemed pleased when he had a hangover.

"It was pretty good. Is the Mate up yet?"

"He's getting up. What time we sailing?"

"Eight o'clock if everyone's aboard. They won't be, of course."

Bervick disappeared. Evans straightened his tie. Then he went below. The Chief and his assistants were at the table when he came into the salon. The Chief seemed cheerful.

"Looks like smooth sailing weather," he observed. He pointed at the window and at the still harbor beyond.

"I hope so." Evans was noncommittal. He had seen too many days when the sea was calm in the harbor

27

and rough outside. They would know the weather soon enough.

Martin and Bervick walked in together.

"Did you get home all right?" Martin asked.

"It looks like it, doesn't it?" Evans spoke sharply. He did not like to be thought a heavy drinker. He noticed Martin was scowling. Evans, deciding that he had spoken too roughly, added, "Yes, the Captain took the Chief and me home. It was some fracas."

Duval laughed loudly. "It sure was! We almost ended up in the ditch a couple times."

"The perils of drink," murmured Martin, his mouth full.

"Not much else to do in these islands," said Evans. He did not really hate the islands, though. They had been home to him before the war when he had fished in these waters. He could not admit to the others, however, that he liked the Aleutians.

"I've got a bad egg," said Bervick. "I guess this was a pre-war egg." He pushed the plate away from him. "I think I'll go get the eight o'clock watch up." He left.

"It takes one to know one," said the Chief, referring back to the eggs.

They ate in silence. The two men on watch entered yawning. They sat down at the other table and started their breakfast. Evans finished his own quickly.

A few minutes before eight, a jeep drove down the dock and stopped at the ship. The three passengers and the Captain climbed out and unloaded their baggage on the dock.

Evans went out on deck. "Good morning," he said.

"It's a hell of a morning," said the Captain. The passengers stood about sheep-like, waiting for guidance. Evans shouted to one of the deckhands inside. Together they got the baggage aboard. Then the passengers and the Captain climbed onto the deck.

The Chaplain hoped that he would not be sick. They all said they hoped they would not be sick. The Major remarked that he had never been seasick in his life; he added, however, that there was a first time for everything. Evans guided them to the dining salon and Martin volunteered to show them to their staterooms. Evans and the Captain went back on deck.

"What's the new report on the outside?" Evans asked.

"According to the man over at Weather and the Navy people, you'll have a ten-foot sea and a thirty-mile wind in gusts from the southwest. That's as far as the Big Harbor. From there you'll have to get another forecast."

"Pretty good news. No planes flying yet?"

"No, no planes. Bad weather beyond the Big Harbor, too." The Captain reached in the coat of his parka and brought out a brown envelope. "Here's your clearance. You can take her away now. Don't spend too much time at Arunga. I don't go for none of that, you know."

Evans smiled. "I know," he said. "We'll be back in a week."

"Fine. Give my love to the Big Harbor girls."

"I sure will."

"Good sailing then." The Captain climbed back on the dock. He stood beside his jeep and waited for them to cast off. Several longshoremen stood by their lines on the dock. The Major and the Chaplain came out to watch and Evans went to the wheelhouse. Martin and Bervick were waiting for him there.

"Cast the bow and spring lines off first. We'll drift out, then let go the stern." He rang the telegraph to the engine room, setting the markers at Stand By. A minute later the engine room rang back. Rather quick for the Chief, he thought. Martin and Bervick went below. Evans could see them, with two deckhands, moving about on deck.

He opened one of the wheelhouse windows. "Let her go," he shouted. Quickly they began to pull in the lines. The bow swung out from the dock.

"Let the stern go, Bervick," he shouted again from the window. A second later they were free of the dock. Evans rang both engines Slow Ahead. Cautiously he maneuvered the ship away from the dock. Then he rang Full Ahead. He could feel the engines vibrate as the ship shot ahead. She would do twelve knots easily.

Martin came up to the wheelhouse. His face was

flushed from the wind and cold and his nose was running. He sniffed as he spoke.

"All squared away. Anything you want done?"

"Nothing I can think of." Evans kept his eyes fixed on the nets that guarded the narrow neck of the harbor a mile away. He steered with the small electrical steering gear. He preferred it to the larger wooden wheel which he insisted that his crew use: it was more seamanlike.

"Guess I'll go to bed then," said Martin, and he went into his cabin. His watch did not begin until noon.

The door opened again and one of the men on Evans' watch entered. He took the wheel and Evans gave him the course from memory. He knew the courses to the Big Harbor by heart.

Ahead he could see the entrance to the nets. He rang Slow Speed as they went through them. The Navy detachment on the near-by point always watched the boats as they passed through, making sure that they were at least at half speed.

Five minutes later they were abeam Andrefski point. The sky was still gray and he could feel the swell of the waves increase beneath them. In a few minutes he would be able to tell how rough the trip would be. He rang Full Speed again.

Bervick came into the wheelhouse. "How's it look to you?" he asked.

"Fair so far," answered Evans. They both looked through the windows at the waves crashing whitely on the black rocks of the point. A haze hung in the air and the wind was not strong or direct. Then they swung around the point and into the open sea. The ship rocked back and forth as she dipped between the swells.

"Just about a ten-foot sea," remarked Bervick.

Evans nodded. "Looks like the forecast is going to be right. Sea striking on the port bow but it doesn't seem so bad. In fact it's pretty good."

"It'll be a good trip." Bervick went into his cabin. Evans stood by the window and watched the bare sharp mountains of the island move slowly by.

"Rather rough, isn't it?"

Evans looked around and saw the Major standing

beside him. The Major was holding onto the wooden railing beneath the window.

"A little bit. We'll make good time, though."

"That's important." The Major looked old this morning, Evans thought. His sallow face showed the signs of heavy drinking. He would probably be sick and say that he had indigestion.

The Major squinted at the mountains. "How far off shore are we?" he asked.

"About two miles. That's our usual running distance."

"It looks closer than that." He contemplated the shifting water and the stone hills and the steel color of the birdless sky. "It looks very close."

"It does," said Evans. The ship was dipping now from sea-valley to sea-mountain with monotonous regularity. Evans was exhilarated by the ship's motion. He felt at home now. This was where he belonged. He began to whistle.

The Major laughed. "I thought that was bad luck—for old mariners to whistle in the wheelhouse."

Evans smiled. "I'm not superstitious."

"Just an old custom, I suppose. Let's hope there's nothing to it."

"There isn't."

They were approaching another cape and Evans gave the man at the wheel a new course.

"Have you been in this business long, Mr Evans?"

"Been at sea long? Well, most of my life, since I was sixteen."

"Really? It must be fascinating." The Major spoke without conviction.

"Yes, it's been a pretty good deal. Sometimes, though, I wish I'd gone to West Point." On an impulse he added this, knowing that it would interest the older man. It did.

"Did you have the opportunity?" he asked.

"In a way. You see the Congressman from our district was a good friend of my uncle who was married to my mother's sister, and I think he could have swung it. I know I used to think about it, but I went to sea instead."

"You made a great mistake," said the Major sadly,

"a very great mistake." He looked out the window as if to behold the proof of the mistake in the rolling sea. Mechanically he made his profile appear hawk-like and military . . . like Wellington. Evans smiled to himself. He had seen a little of the regular army people and he thought them all alike. To parade around in uniform and live on an uncomfortable army post, to play poker and gossip; that was all of the world to them, he thought. The life wasn't bad, of course, but one was not one's own boss and there was not, naturally, the sea. The life seemed dull to him.

"I suppose it was a mistake," said Evans, knowing it was not.

The Major sighed, "I can't say that I care very much for the water." His face was drawn and tired and there were gravish pouches under his eyes.

"It's something you have to have in you, I guess. With me it was being a sailor or a farmer. Farming was hard work and so I got to be a sailor."

"Sometimes one shouldn't run away from the hard things," said Major Barkison tightly. "The easy way is not always the best way," he added with infinite wisdom.

"I guess you're right at that."

"Well, I think I shall go downstairs now." The Major walked unsteadily across the rocking wheelhouse deck. He opened the door and went below.

"Quite a guy, the Major," the man at the wheel remarked.

"Yes, he seems to be O.K. At least he's not chicken like some of the ones we've carried."

"No, he seems to be a good guy."

Evans looked out the window. The weather was consistent. The wind was blowing around twenty miles an hour. There was a thick snow flurry a few miles ahead. He would go by the clock through the snow.

The wheelhouse was quiet. From other parts of the ship he could hear voices, and from the galley came the occasional sounds of breaking china.

The clock struck three bells. Snow began to splatter on the window glass and whiten the decks. He could see only a few yards ahead. The sea had gotten no rougher, though, and the wind was dying down. He looked out into the whiteness and thought of nothing.

Martin came out of his cabin. "How's it going?" he asked.

"Pretty good. Some snow just came up. We'll be off Point Kada in five minutes."

"That's good time. Want me to take over for a while?"

Evans was surprised. Martin usually slept until his watch began at noon. It was unusual for him to be helpful. "Sure. Fine. Thanks," he said, and he went below.

The cook was swearing at the stove. The pots slid dangerously back and forth over the stove. Evans passed quickly through the galley.

In the salon the Chaplain and the young Lieutenant sat. There was an open book on the Chaplain's lap, but he did not seem to have been reading. He appeared ill. Lieutenant Hodges on the other hand was enjoying himself. He was watching the waves hit against the stern.

The salon was lighted by one electric bulb. Everything looked shapeless in the sickly light: the rack where the tattered library of the ship was kept, the wooden chairs piled on the two tables, the two men sitting in one corner, all this looked gloomy and strange to him. He flipped on another light and the place became cheerful.

"Quite unpleasant, isn't this?" Chaplain O'Mahoney remarked. He closed the book on his lap.

"Beginning to feel it?"

"Oh my no, certainly not. I've been sitting here reading. I feel very well."

"Where's the Major?"

Lieutenant Hodges answered, "He's asleep in his stateroom. I think he's pretty tired after last night."

"So I gather. You went home early, didn't you, Chaplain?"

"Yes, yes, I had to get my eight hours, you know," he said lightly. "I had so many things to do before our departure."

Evans turned toward the galley. "Hey, Smitty!" he shouted. "When you going to have chow?"

"In about a hour."

"See you then." Evans nodded to the two men and went back to the wheelhouse. Martin was looking out the window and singing softly to himself. Evans stood beside him. They watched the snow swirling over the water; they watched for signs of change. That's all this business was, thought Evans. Watching the sea and guessing what it might do next. The mist was thinning, he noticed. He could make out a familiar cape ahead of them. They were on course.

"How's your buddy, the Major?" asked Martin.

"He's in his sack."

"I thought he was up here for a while."

"He was."

"I guess you'll make Chief Warrant now."

Evans flushed, "That's your department, polishing the brass."

"You do it so much better." Martin chuckled. Evans bit his lip. He knew that Martin often tried to irritate him and he did not like it when he succeeded. He turned away from him. The man at the wheel had been listening and was grinning.

Evans looked at the compass without seeing the numbers. "Keep to your course."

"But I am on course," the man said righteously.

Evans grunted. Martin walked away from the window and back into his cabin. Evans cursed slightly. Then, relieved, he stood, looking out the port window, his arms and legs braced as the ship plunged from wave to wave, slanting the wheelhouse deck.

At five bells Smitty shouted that chow was ready.

Evans went into the mates' cabin. Both were asleep. He shook Bervick, who was in the top bunk.

"Lunch. You'd better get up." Bervick groaned and Martin rolled out of the lower bunk.

"You take over," Evans said, speaking to Martin. "You can eat when I get back. I'll take part of your watch for you." He went below.

The crew was using the galley table. The officers and

passengers used one of the salon tables. The three passengers were walking about aimlessly.

"All ready for some of our wonderful hash?" Evans spoke the words gaily, but even to his own ears they sounded flat. He did not have Martin's light touch with words.

"I feel quite hungry," said the Major, rubbing his hands together briskly.

"I seem to have no appetite," said the Chaplain sadly. They sat down at the table. The Major on Evans' right, the Chaplain on his left. Hodges sat next to Duval, who had come up from the engine room.

"Engines running smoothly, Chief?" Evans asked.

Duval beamed. "They've never been better. We're making good time."

"Good." Evans helped himself to the hash. It looked pale and unnourishing. The Major frowned.

"This is that new canned ration, isn't it?"

"Yes. We have this when we're traveling. It's usually too rough to have anything else fixed."

"I see." The Major took some. The Chaplain decided that he was not hungry at all.

"You had better have some crackers," Evans remarked. The Chaplain refused with a weary smile.

There was little conversation. Bervick and the Chief disagreed on the expected time of arrival. For a moment Evans was afraid they would begin an involved argument. Luckily they had enough sense not to. Evans wondered why people could never get along with each other. Of course living in too close quarters for a long time had a lot to do with it. On these boats people saw too much of one another.

After lunch Evans went back to the wheelhouse. Silently he relieved Martin who went below. There was another snow flurry ahead. It looked as if the rest of the trip would be by the clock. Evans watched the water and waited for the snow to come.

At noon Martin returned.

"Where are we?" he asked.

Evans studied the pale snow-blurred coast. "Almost abeam Crown rock. We'll be in the Big Harbor in about two hours. Don't get any closer to shore than we are and wake me up when you think you're near the nets."

"O.K." Martin checked the compass and the log-book and then he stood by the window and looked out. Evans went into his cabin and stretched out on his bunk. The rocking of the boat he found soothing. He slept.

*   *   *   *

"We're about two miles from the nets," said Martin, when Evans came back into the wheelhouse. Outside the snow was thick and they could see nothing but a blinding whiteness. The outline of the shore was gone. Evans checked the time and the chart. He figured that they were less than two miles from the entrance buoy. In another ten minutes they should be able to see the nets. He rang Stand By. Martin went below and Evans waited for a thinning of the snow.

At last it came. Dimly he could see the great black mass of mountain that marked the entrance to the Big Harbor. He felt much better seeing this. He had never lost a ship in the fog or snow, but he knew that far better sailors than he had gone on the rocks in similar weather.

He directed the man at the wheel to pull in closer to shore. Just ahead of him, only somewhat hazed by the thinning snow, he could make out a red buoy off his starboard bow. Beyond this buoy were the nets. He rang for Half Speed. On the deck below he could see the Major standing in the wind. The Major thought Evans looked quite nautical, as he gazed sternly into the snow. Spray splashing over the bow sent him quick-ly to cover.

At Slow Speed, Evans glided the ship between the nets. For five minutes they vibrated slowly ahead. Then, in the near distance, he suddenly saw the spires of the old Russian church, rising above the native village.

To the right of the village were the docks. Evans took the wheel himself and the ship moved slowly around the harbor's only reef. With a quick spin of the wheel Evans took the ship in closer to shore. The water was deep up to within a few feet of the black abbreviated beach. A hundred yards ahead of them were the docks.

Two deckhands stood on the bow and attached heaving lines to the bow and spring lines. Martin stood by the anchor winch, his eyes on the dock where they would tie up. No other ships were on the face of this dock. They would have it to themselves.

Evans stopped both engines. They drifted ahead. The wind was off their port bow, which was good. He pointed the bow toward the center of the dock and then he waited.

Ten feet from the dock he began to swing the bow away from shore. He swore loudly as the ship turned too slowly. He had mistimed the speed. Quickly he gave the off shore engine Slow Astern. The bow pulled out more quickly, while the stern swung in. They hit lightly against the pilings. A man on shore had already taken their spring line. Evans stopped the off shore engine and waited to see if the lines were under control. They were and he rang off the engine room. The landing had been good. His heart was fluttering, he noticed, and the sweat trickled down his left side. These landings were a strain.

ii

Martin was in his bunk; handling the lines had tired him. His eyes were shut but he was not asleep. He listened to Bervick moving about the cabin. "Going up town?" he asked.

"That's right." Bervick adjusted his cap.

"You going to see Olga?"

"I might. Haven't had much to do with her lately."

"That's right, you haven't."

Bervick pulled on his parka. Thinking of Olga excited him. He still liked her, and the thought of the Chief with her, bothered him. The Chief would not be with her tonight; for some reason he was sure of that. Tonight was his night.

"I'll be seeing you," he said to Martin, and he went out onto the forward deck.

The tide was going out and the wheelhouse was now level with the dock. With an effort he pulled himself up to the dock. To his left was the native village and to his right were more docks and warehouses. Men from the various boats walked about on shore, dim figures in the twilight. Pale blue smoke circled up from the galley smokestacks. There was a smell of cooking, of supper, in the cool air. Bervick turned and walked into the village.

The main street of the settlement curved parallel with the beach for half a mile. Most of the houses were on this street. Bars and restaurants and one theater, all wooden, also lined the street. The buildings had been painted white originally; they were many weathered shades of gray, now. On a small hill, behind two bars and a former brothel, the old Russian Orthodox church rose straightly against the evening. Its two onion-shaped cupolas were painted green; the rest of the church was an almost new white.

On several lanes, running inland from the main street, were the homes of the two hundred odd pre-war residents. Most of the houses had been vacated at the beginning of the war. The windows were boarded up and the privies leaned crazily in the back yards. Seven trees, which had been imported, were withered now, and their limbs had been made grotesque by the constant wind.

A mile inland from the shore and the village was the army camp. It had been erected early in the war and its many barracks and offices duplicated the military life of the distant United States.

Soldiers from the post and sailors from the Navy ships in the harbor wandered about the crooked lanes and along the main street. They were looking for liquor and women. There was much of one and little of the other in the Big Harbor. Prices were high for both.

Bervick walked very slowly down the main street, proving to himself that he was in no hurry to see Olga. He would see her later in the evening.

He stopped at a building somewhat larger than the rest. It was the Arctic Commercial Store, the main store in the village. Almost anything could be bought here. It was said that the store had made over a million dollars since the war.

Bervick went inside. It was warm and crowded and cheerful. Sailors with beards in various stages of development walked about. Some wore gold earrings in their ears. Bervick grimaced. Earrings were an old sea custom recently revived. He did not like them.

The shelves of the store were stocked with canned goods and souvenirs; upstairs was a clothing store. Bervick looked around at the counters. In the corner where souvenirs were sold, he saw several bright pink and blue silk pillow covers. On them were printed, in gay colors, maps of Alaska and various endearments.

"How much is that one there?" Bervick asked the bearded man behind the counter.

"What one?"

"That one over there." Bervick flushed and pointed to a pink one, inscribed *To My Sweetheart*.

"You mean the Sweetheart one?" Bervick wondered if the man were deaf. For some reason he felt a little foolish. He nodded and said, "Yes, that's the one."

The bearded man chuckled and handed it to him. Bervick paid him. The price was too high but that was not unusual here.

He stuffed the fake silk cover in his pocket. When he saw Olga he would give it to her casually. The Chief had more money, but sometimes sentiment was much more important. His breath came shorter when he thought of Olga. He controlled himself. He would not go to her yet. She had probably already heard that his ship was in. He would make her wait for him. Bervick hoped the Chief would not try to see her tonight. The Chief had said that he planned to work on the engines. Bervick hoped that he would. The Chief wasn't really much competition, though, thought Bervick.

He walked down the street. Drunken sailors in groups went grimly from bar to bar. The Shore Patrol men stood warily on the wooden sidewalk, waiting for trouble. Fights would begin later in the evening.

The Anchorage Inn was a popular bar. It rambled for a hundred feet or less on the main street, a few buildings from the Arctic Commercial Store. Bervick decided to have a drink.

A blast of heat and light engulfed him as he entered. The smell of liquor, food, and too many people was strong in the room. It took him several minutes to get used to the light and heat.

A long counter extended across one end of the building. Through the open kitchen door, behind the counter, he could see a fat woman cooking at a greasy stove; clouds of smoke and steam sizzled up from the stove. Two women and one man were serving at the counter and tables. Soldiers and sailors crowded the place. A half-dozen women were unevenly distributed. They worked in the shops and restaurants and bars. They made a lot of money.

Sitting at a table with two sailors was a large woman who immediately recognized Bervick. "Hey, Joe," she yelled. "You come over here."

"Hello, Angela. How're you doing?" Bervick sat down at the table. The two sailors were young and seemed frightened by Angela. They looked relieved to see him.

Angela was a huge and heavy breasted woman. She wore a green dress of thick cloth. Her eyes were narrow puffy slits and her face was painted carelessly. There was no reason for her to take pains up here, thought Bervick. Any woman was a beauty to men who had been without women for many months and occasionally years. Her hair was a bright brass red, dark at the roots. Angela was several years older than the forty she claimed to be.

"What's new, Joe?" she asked when he had made himself comfortable.

"Not a thing. We just got in a little while ago."

"Yeah. I heard."

"News travels fast, I guess."

"It sure does."

The two young sailors mumbled something and moved away. Angela winked, "There they go . . . my admirers."

"I guess you still got a lot of them."

"Oh, I don't do so bad. When you going to visit me? I live over the store now, you know."

"So I heard."

"News travels fast." They laughed.

"How's little Olga?" Angela asked.

"I suppose she's O.K. I don't see her so much any more."

"That's just as well. I don't like to talk much about the other girls, you know I don't, but that Olga is just plain loose. I'm not saying the rest of us are any the better, I mean I know I'm not such a pure . . . well, you know, but after all I don't take on more than one. . . ."

"For Christ's sake!" Bervick snapped at her. He was disgusted by this corrupt mass of a woman saying such a thing of Olga. "That's hard to believe," he added more calmly.

"What? That I don't go with more than one? Why you know perfectly well I don't. My only fault is that I'm just too affectionate." She purred this last, and under the table her knee was pushed against his.

"I guess that's right." You couldn't be angry with Angela, he thought. He wondered if Olga would be waiting for him.

"Then of course you know about her . . . Olga, I mean . . . two-timing that Frenchman off your boat. What's his name?"

"I know about that. That's old." Bervick spoke with authority, and Angela was impressed as he intended her to be.

"Well, maybe she's through with him." She sighed and her great breasts rippled. Bervick wondered if Olga might marry him if he asked her. That would certainly cut the Chief out, he thought viciously. He frowned.

"What's the matter, darling?" asked Angela, leaning over the table, her face close to his. Cheap perfume floated up from her in heavy waves; it made him want to cough.

"Not a thing, Angela, not a thing." He moved back in his chair.

"Well, don't frown so," she said peevishly, and then more brightly, "What about a drink? They've got some good stuff here. Hey, Joe," she yelled at the waiter. He came over to their table.

"Two shots, Joe."

The man went behind the counter and returned a moment later with two jiggers of whiskey. Bervick started to pay.

"Never mind." Angela pushed his money aside. "This is on the house, isn't it, Joe?"

"Sure." Joe walked away.

"I know so many things about Joe, you see." Angela giggled. They gulped the whiskey. A tall blond sailor across the room caught her eye. She smiled and winked at him. The sailor came over to their table.

"Hello, beautiful," he said.

"Hello, handsome." Angela made fluttering feminine movements. Bervick stood up.

"I think I'll go now," he said. He noticed the sailor wore a gold earring in one of his ears.

"Bad luck, soldier," said the sailor, leering and putting his arm around Angela. Bervick turned away.

"Give my best to Olga," said Angela. He did not answer. He walked outside into the cold air of the Arctic night. The whiskey had warmed him and he did not feel the cold. He was glad he had taken it.

The street was crowded with sailors. They were becoming more noisy. Bervick walked on the extreme edge of the road in the shadow of the buildings. He wanted no trouble tonight.

The restaurant where Olga worked was called the Fall Inn. It was owned by a man named Fall who had a great sense of humor. Olga used to laugh a lot with Bervick when she thought of the funny name Mr Fall had thought of. She liked to explain to customers why the name of the restaurant was so funny.

The Fall Inn was a large, well-lighted frame house on one of the lanes that went back from the main street. Near it was a withered evergreen tree surrounded by a picket fence. This had been Mrs Fall's idea.

Bervick stepped inside. He stood in the doorway, accustoming his eyes to the light. Behind the counter stood Olga. She was waiting on a dozen or so customers. Olga was a tall girl with a slim figure. Her features were rather flat and without distinction, but her eyes were a beautiful shiny china blue. Her hair was silver-gold, long and untidy, and her complexion was white and smooth. She had thick legs and graceful hands.

She saw Bervick when he came in. She looked away quickly and busied herself with the cash register.

He went over to her and sat down at the counter. "How are you?" he asked, not knowing anything else to say.

"What do you want?" She spoke nervously.

"I just wanted to see you," he said. "I guess it's O.K. for me to sit here."

"Go ahead, it's a public place." Still she did not go away. A man across the room shouted for some coffee. Slowly she went back into the kitchen. She seemed frightened.

"Not making any headway with her, are you?" Bervick looked behind him. Duval was standing there. He had been there for some time.

Bervick felt sick to his stomach. For a moment he said nothing. Then he asked easily, "What are you doing here?" He was careful to control his voice.

"Just what do you think, Sergeant?" Duval grinned. "I'm just here having some coffee and maybe having Olga later on. I haven't made up my mind yet." Duval sat down beside him.

"I thought," Bervick spoke slowly, "that you weren't going to see her tonight."

"I never said I wasn't. Besides it's her and my business. She don't want nothing to do with you anyway."

"That's where you're wrong."

"Well, you just go ask her, sucker." Duval played with the sugar container.

Olga came back from the kitchen. She was frowning. Her light brows almost met.

"What are you doing tonight? Are you going to see this guy?" Bervick asked. Olga flushed and thought a moment. Bervick knew already what she would answer. Olga liked money too well. But, knowing this, he still wanted her.

Olga decided to be angry. "What makes you two

think you're so good you can tell me what to do? I think you're both conceited. Maybe I ain't interested in neither of you."

"Maybe you're right," said Duval. "I guess I'll just pay for some coffee and get on out." Then he opened his wallet and let her see the thick sheaf of bills. Her eyes narrowed.

"What you in such a hurry to go for? My gracious, you'd think I was poison or something." A customer yelled for food and she went back into the kitchen.

"I'd like to break your back," said Bervick very deliberately, making each word a curse.

"Don't get upset, Sergeant. I just got more than you. I been keeping Olga ever since she got tired of you. You know that, so why do you keep hanging around? What you want to do? Marry her?"

Bervick felt sick. He watched the Chief's wide mouth move as he spoke. He noticed the Chief had a bright gold upper tooth. It gleamed cheerfully as he spoke.

Duval went on talking. "There's some other girls around here. What about that fat girl who's so stuck on you? What's her name? Angela?"

"Angela!" exclaimed Olga. She came back from the kitchen in time to hear the name "Angela." "Why she's just a big fat you-know-what. So you been seeing her." She turned on Bervick, glad at last of an excuse to be rid of him. "Well, you got your nerve to want to do anything with me after you been with her. Why I bet she's got everything wrong with her." A customer wanted to pay for his meal. She went to the cash register.

"Too bad," said Duval. "You aren't much of a lover, are you? You go see Angela. She's just your speed."

Unsteadily Bervick got to his feet. He buttoned his parka. Olga did not look at him; she pretended to be busy figuring change. The Chief absently twirled the sugar container between his broad hands.

Bervick walked out of the Fall Inn. He did not shiver when the cold hit him. Some men from the boats were urinating beside one of the buildings. They did it all the time, all over the place. It was unpleasant, he thought.

Someone should put a stop to it. Thinking of this and not of Olga, he walked back to the Anchorage Inn.

Angela was not surprised to see him. The blond sailor with the gold earring was sound asleep in the chair beside her. On the table was a half empty bottle of whiskey. Wearily Bervick walked over to her.

"Hello, darling," she said brightly. "Was Olga mean to you?"

"That's right," he said. He sat down beside her. The sailor stirred sleepily. His long hair fell in his face.

"Nice, isn't he?" commented Angela, with a motherly air.

"Yeah. What are you doing tonight?"

She looked at him. The playfulness left her face. She was strictly business now. "Sure, darling, sure," she said. "But you know how it is."

"I know just how it is. I only got ten dollars," he lied.

Angela sighed. Then she smiled, her fat face creased with kindness. "I'll lose my reputation for this," she said with a chuckle, "but for an old pal, that's a deal." Bervick thanked her. He wondered to himself how these wrecks of women would ever be able to adjust themselves to peacetime when no man would look at them. "Of course you might take me to the show first," she added coquettishly: a female elephant trembling at the thought of love.

"I suppose I could. What's on tonight?"

"*Saturday Magic*. I hear it's real good. I saw it advertised when I was in Frisco ten years ago."

"That sounds good to me." Bervick helped her up. The sailor was still asleep. Angela took the bottle of whiskey and slipped it in her coat pocket.

"He'll never miss it. Besides we might want some in the movie," she said cozily. They pushed their way through the crowd of soldiers and sailors. Standing outside the door were two Shore Patrol men waiting gloomily for the eventual riot.

"Nasty bunch them SP's," remarked Angela, and then, "Jesus but it's cold." She pulled her coat tight about her neck. Quickly they walked to the small theater at the end of the street.

The theater held about two hundred people. It was almost filled now and the show had begun. They found seats at the back. A shot was being fired on the screen and Angela, hearing it, squealed with gay terror. Two rows in front of them a man vomited. Bervick shuddered.

"That's all right, dear. You'll be warm in a minute," whispered Angela. He put his arm around her thick shoulders. She giggled and let her hand rest on his knee. Together they watched the figures on the screen and thought of each other.

iii

Morning came whitely over the harbor. The water was oily calm. A small Navy boat went through the channel and the crews of the different boats began to stir about on the docks.

Bervick walked down the deserted street of the village. The houses looked unlived in. There was no sign of life away from the docks. His footsteps sounded sharp and clear in the emptiness of the morning.

He thought of Angela and felt sick at the memory of her making love in a torn silk dressing gown, her frizzled red hair hanging stiffly down her back. Olga was so much cleaner. He would not think of Olga, though.

The ship was already awake. The crew was straggling up out of the focs'le. He could see Evans moving around in the wheelhouse. Martin was out on the forward deck.

"Have a good time?" yelled Martin when he saw him.

"Sure. Don't I always?"

"Sure."

Bervick climbed aboard and stood beside Martin who was adjusting the hatch cover.

"Who were you with last night? Olga?"

"No. I was with Angela."

"That pig?"

"I know it." Bervick sighed and began, for the first

time, to recall Angela's large torso. "She's got a nice personality," he said absently.

"Don't they all?" said Martin. He kicked the edge of the canvas into place. "Let's have chow."

Evans was sitting alone at the table when they came in. He muttered a good morning. They sat down.

Bervick was hungry. He ate even the cold-storage eggs, which Smitty invariably served them and which they seldom ate.

Martin looked up. "Say, Evans," he said, "what's this story I hear about John Jones? You know, the Indian guy from Seldovia."

"He killed himself." Evans pushed himself back from the table and teetered his chair on the deck.

"What went wrong?" Bervick was interested. He had been on a power barge with Jones.

"He drank a bottle of methyl alcohol last night." Evans made himself appear bored. He always did when anyone they knew died.

"Well, what did he do that for?" Evans irritated Bervick sometimes. Evans always wanted to be asked things, as if he were an authority.

"The girl he had back in Seldovia, an Indian girl, she left him and gets married. She writes him about it and he locks himself up in the head and drinks this stuff. They found him around midnight. He looked pretty awful they said. I guess he took the girl too seriously." Bervick knew the last remark was intended for him and he did not like it. He would not kill himself for a woman, not himself, that was certain.

"That's life," said Martin helpfully. The Chaplain and the Major entered the salon. Both were cheerful and both looked rested. They announced that young Hodges was still asleep.

"We played poker for a little while last night. Where were you, Sergeant? We needed an extra man." The Major spoke genially to show that aboard ship he was not conscious of rank.

"I was visiting friends in the village, sir." Bervick shifted uneasily in his chair.

"They have a fine old Russian church there, don't they?" asked the Chaplain.

"Yes, they do."

"Very interesting, these old churches. I suppose one can't go in the church here."

"I think it's locked until the war's over," said Evans. "The priest was evacuated."

"Such a pity," the Chaplain complained. "I should like to have seen it."

Duval and his assistants came up from the engine room. The first assistant, a short heavy man, was splattered with grease.

"What's the matter?" Evans asked.

"Just a little trouble with the auxiliary again. It'll be O.K. I think. Just go easy on them winches. I been up since five working on this damned thing." Duval gestured with his hands. Bervick wondered when he had left Olga.

"Good morning, Bervick," said Duval genially. "Did you sleep well last night?"

Without answering Bervick left the salon and went in the galley. He could hear the Major murmur words of surprise and he could hear Evans change the subject.

Martin joined Bervick in the wheelhouse. "What's bothering you?" he asked. "You aren't still sore at the Chief because of that Norwegian animal?"

"Maybe I am. That's my business."

"You're acting like a half-wit. Before you know it, the Chief'll get Evans to throw you off the boat."

"That's fine by me. I don't know if I want to be around that guy." Bervick gave the bulkhead a vicious poke.

"You're getting a little crazy in the head."

Bervick shrugged. "I'm not the only one, I guess."

"Well, you better not bother the Chief very much or there'll be some real trouble one of these days. Anyway I can't see how you managed to get so hot and bothered over Olga."

"That's my business."

Martin looked at Bervick and saw that there were harsh lines about his mouth. He was fingering his long hair.

"I guess it is," said Martin finally.

Evans came whistling into the wheelhouse. He was

followed by a Captain, the Assistant Superintendent of the harbor.

"Are we sailing?" asked Martin.

Evans nodded. "Just as soon as the Captain here gives us clearance."

"The weather . . . ?"

"According to the Navy," said the Captain, examining some papers in his hand, "according to the Navy you will encounter heavy weather near the Agan cape. Twenty-foot sea at the worst. Fair visibility and not too much wind. Of course you realize at this time of year anything can happen."

"There are no planes leaving, are there?" asked Evans.

The Captain shook his head. "Not for a week anyway. This is about the quickest trip for the Major." He handed Evans an envelope. "Here's your clearance and the weather report in detail. See you on your way back." The Captain left.

"We're off," said Martin. He looked out over the still harbor. "I guess it will be a good trip. Hope so, anyway."

Evans looked at the gray sky. "There's a lot of snow up there. Go tell the Major that he can't fly. He wanted to know."

Martin and Bervick went below together. They found the Major in the salon, filing his nails. He looked inquiringly at them.

"No planes leaving, sir," said Martin. "They're still weathered in."

"Well, that *is* too bad." The Major seemed cheerful. Bervick decided that Major Barkison liked the idea of a three-day trip. "Will we leave soon?"

"Right away."

"Good."

Bervick and Martin met the Chaplain in the companionway. The Chaplain was not particularly pleased at the idea of a boat trip, but he decided to be hearty and take it like a good sport. "Well, that will be nice. I have always wanted to do this sort of thing. We never were near the ocean in Maryland. That is, Maryland was near, or rather on, the ocean, but we weren't. This'll be quite an experience for a landsman."

"It will," said Martin.

"I hope I shan't have a repeat performance. . . ."

"Not if you eat plenty of crackers. Will you excuse us, Chaplain?"

"Of course."

They could hear Evans ringing Stand By. Together they went out on deck. The men on watch were already there.

"How do you want to go?" Martin shouted to Evans in the wheelhouse. Evans put his head out the window.

"Let everything go at once!"

Two seamen from one of the power barges stood by their lines on the dock.

"O.K.," said Martin. "Cast off." The crew began to pull in the lines. Bervick went aft and helped handle the stern. Martin waited while the men coiled the lines. Then he yelled to Evans, "All free!" He could see Evans nod and go to the telegraph.

The ship swung slowly away from the dock. The wind blew damply and gently in their faces. The sea gulls circled high overhead.

Bervick joined Martin on the forward deck. They watched the bow of the ship cut with increasing speed through the dark and rippled water.

"It looks awful quiet, don't it, Martin?"

"Does look quiet. I hope it stays that way. The weather didn't look too good in the report."

"Didn't look bad?"

"No."

"I wish to hell I'd stayed in the Merchant Marine."

"It's tough all over."

"Yeah."

"We better see what Evans wants. He'll probably want to hose down the decks."

"Yeah."

As they turned to go, Bervick reached in his pocket and brought out a bundle which he tossed quickly overboard.

"What was that?" asked Martin curiously.

"Some old rags."

"Oh." They went below.

The bow of the ship cut more and more swiftly through the harbor and toward the nets. The gulls wheeled higher and higher in the sky, and on the crest of one wave floated a pink piece of cloth, decorated with the words *To My Sweetheart* . . . and a map of Alaska.

Chapter Three

i

MAJOR BARKISON contemplated the sea and was pleased by it. Today the water was smooth and only occasionally disturbed by gusts of wind. The Major stood alone on the forward deck. A few miles to his left was the vanishing entrance to the Big Harbor; before him was the Bering Sea.

Dreamily the Major thought of the sea: of the great masses of moon-guided water, constantly shifting: of sunken ships; of all the centuries that people had gone out on the water, and of all those, like Evans, to whom the sea was a part of living. He enjoyed thinking of these large vague things as the ship moved steadily ahead, causing sharp small waves of its own, waves which shattered themselves into the larger ones.

The water of the Bering Sea was a deep blue-black, thought the Major, and he watched carefully the ship-made waves: black when with the sea mass, then varying shades of clear blue as they swept up into the large waves, exploding at last in sudden whiteness. When he had the time, Major Barkison appreciated beauty. He had three days now in which to be appreciative.

Several sea lions wallowed fearlessly near the ship. Their black coats glistened in the pale morning light. For a moment they dove and splashed near the ship, and then, quickly, they went away.

He heard the sound of wings behind him. He turned and saw the Indian cook throwing garbage overboard. The air was filled with sea gulls, fighting for scraps on the water. He watched them as they glided in the air,

52

their wings motionless, their heads rigidly pointed. They seemed reptilian to him. For the first time, noticing their unblinking black beady eyes, he saw the snake in these smooth gray birds. The Major did not like snakes.

Visibility was good. They seemed even closer than two miles to shore. In the distance, toward the end of the island, he could see one of the active volcanos. At regular intervals a column of smoke and fire came up out of it. The island was a cluster of volcanos, tall and sharp, their peaks covered with snow. Clouds hung over the peaks and the stone of the mountains was black and gray.

Overhead the sun made an effort to shine through the clouded sky; the sun seldom did, though. This was the place where the bad weather was made, according to the Indians, and the Major agreed. He yawned and was glad that he had not flown. He did not like flying over hidden peaks. He hoped this trip would be uneventful.

Major Barkison had a sure method of foretelling weather, or anything else for that matter. He would, for instance, select a certain patch of sky and then count slowly to three; if, during that time, no sea gull crossed the patch of sky, the thing he wanted would come true. This method could be applied to everything and the Major had great faith in it.

He looked at a section of sky above a distant volcano. Slowly he counted. At the count of two a gull flew across his patch of sky. The Major frowned. He had a way, however, of dealing with this sort of thing. He would use the best two counts out of three. Quickly he counted. No gull appeared. The trip would not be bad. In his mind, though, he wondered if it might not be cheating to take the best two out of three. One had to play fair. Not that he was superstitious, of course.

The Major began to feel the cold of the wind. The cold came gradually. He did not realize it until he found himself shivering. Carefully, holding onto the railing, he walked aft to the galley.

Inside he stood by the range and warmed himself. He shivered as the cold left. Steam came up from his hands.

Hodges and the Chaplain were sitting at the galley table drinking coffee. The Indian cook was arranging some canned rations in a cupboard. Major Barkison took off his parka and sat down at the galley table.

"Pretty cold, isn't it?" remarked the Chaplain.

"Yes, it is. Very penetrating, this cold. Goes right through to the bone."

"I suppose so. Actually this isn't half so cold as Anchorage or Nome. The Chain isn't much worse than Seattle."

"I'll take Seattle," said Hodges. "Who was it who said this place was the chamber pot of the gods?" The Major laughed.

"I hear," said the Chaplain, "that you are going to be promoted, Major."

"How did you hear that?"

The Chaplain giggled. "Through the grapevine. You hear all sorts of things that way, you know."

Barkison nodded. "It looks like it'll be coming through any time now."

"That'll be nice for you. Your career and all that."

"Yes, it will be nice." The Major poured himself a cup of coffee from the pot on the stove. Then he sat down again. He poured some canned milk into the coffee.

"They say that the natives think that's where milk comes from, out of a can," Hodges remarked.

"You can get to like condensed milk," said the Major. "I never used to like it before I came up here." He stirred his coffee and thought of Fort Lewis where he had been stationed for many years before the war. As he remembered, he missed the trees and green fields the most; large leafy trees and green smooth clover pastures. He wondered how long it would be before he went back.

"Where is your home?" asked the Chaplain, turning to Hodges.

"Virginia, the northern part."

"Oh, really. That's quite near to me. You know the monastery of Saint Oliver?" Hodges shook his head. "Well that's where I was, near Baltimore, you know. When I was a child I used to visit relatives in Pikefield County. You didn't know anyone in Pikefield, did you?"

"I'm afraid I never did. I was never in the southern part of the state much. I was mostly in Fairfax."

"Great country," commented the Major. "I've been in many horse shows around there, around Warrenton. Beautiful country, I've always liked it."

"I never knew you rode, sir," said Hodges.

"Why yes. I was in the cavalry when I first got out of the Point. Changed over later. Cavalry was a little bit too much wear and tear for me. You see," and he lowered his voice and spoke rather wearily, "you see, I have a heart murmur."

"Really?" The Chaplain became interested. "Isn't that odd, but you know I've got the same thing. As a matter of fact the doctor up at Anchorage told me I might drop dead at any moment. You can imagine how surprised I was to hear that."

"I can imagine." The Major spoke drily. The Chaplain's heart did not interest him. He was a little annoyed that the Chaplain should have mentioned it.

"Yes, I might drop dead at any moment." Chaplain O'Mahoney seemed to enjoy saying those words.

The Major looked out the porthole and watched the gray water shifting under the still sunless sky.

"I like Anchorage," said the Chaplain absently.

"The best place in Alaska," agreed Hodges. "You can get real steak there. You got to pay high for it, though."

"Sure, but they're a lot more civilized than some places I could mention. It certainly does get cold up there." The Chaplain shuddered at the thought.

"That's why war is hell," said the Major. He wondered how long it would be before his promotion came through. Almost without thinking he used his method. If the Chaplain blinked his eyes within the count of three, he would not get his promotion for at least six months. He looked at the Chaplain's eyes and he counted to himself. The Chaplain did not blink. Major Barkison felt much better. He would be a Lt Colonel in less than six months. O'Mahoney was watching him, he noticed.

"Do you feel well, Major?" the Chaplain asked.

"Never better. Why?"

"I thought you looked odd. You were staring so. It must be my imagination."

"It must be. I was just staring, daydreaming, you know."

"Yes, I do it often myself. Once I had an unusual revelation that way."

The Major changed the subject. He spoke to Hodges. "Are you going to stay with the Adjutant General's department after the war?" Lieutenant Hodges was regular army like the Major.

Hodges shook his head. "I don't think so. I'm going to try to get in Operations."

"It's quite interesting, these revelations; I suppose one would call them that. . . ." O'Mahoney began again.

Major Barkison interrupted hurriedly. "I am certain they are." He turned to the Lieutenant. "Of course, Hodges, the work's quite different from what you've been doing."

"I know. I think I'd like it though."

Barkison could see that O'Mahoney was trying to decide whether to tell of his revelation or not. He decided not to. They sat without speaking, and the Major listened to the sounds of the ship. Distant voices from the salon and the wheelhouse and, nearer them, the soft curses of Smitty, the Indian cook, as he prepared lunch. The ship, Barkison noticed, was rocking more than usual. Evans was probably changing course.

The Major excused himself and walked into the almost dark salon and stood by the after door, looking out. In shallow ridges the wake of the ship foamed on the sky-gray water: gray when you looked at its surface but obsidian-dark beneath. A slight wind blew, troubling only the gulls, who floated uneasily on it.

Martin came and stood beside him in the doorway.

"Ah, Mr Martin. Smooth sailing, isn't it?"

"Yes, very."

"I'm certainly glad it is. Certainly glad it's calm. I had thought we might have rough weather according to the report, but it doesn't seem so."

"Might be bad yet, Major. This is pretty unusual. In fact this isn't at all what we expected."

"Weather's incalculable here, I suppose. That's true of all the Aleutians, I suppose."

"You're right there. You can't tell much till it's almost too late."

"What sort of work did you do before you came in the army, if I may ask?"

"I was an actor."

"Is that so?" At one time the Major had been interested in the theater. He was still fascinated by the business. "Were you in the pictures?"

"No, on the stage. Up around New England."

"Indeed? This," the Major pointed at the water, "this seems quite different from that sort of work."

"In a way I suppose so. That's what the army does. It's just one of those things, I guess."

"Just one of those things," echoed the Major. He thought of himself on a stage. In his mind he could see himself playing Wellington. The uniforms would be flattering. He would look martial in them. Major Barkison was a romantic, a frustrated romantic perhaps, but still a romantic. Before the war, when the army could wear civilian clothes, Major Barkison had worn very bright ties. "Must be interesting work."

"Yes, I guess I'll do it again if I can."

"You must certainly. One should always do the thing one does best." The Major spoke with the firmness of the master of the platitude.

"That's right, sir."

Major Barkison toyed with the thought of himself as Wellington. The thought was pleasant and he examined it from all angles. He dreamed for several moments.

"I understand," said Martin at last, "that they are going to rotate to the States all men who've been here two years or more."

"What? Oh, yes, that's our policy. It's a little hard to do, naturally. There aren't many replacements so far. How long have you been here?"

"Fourteen months. I've got another ten months to go."

"I know how you feel. How long has Mr Evans been here?"

"Over three years, but then he's practically a native. He lived in Seward. He probably likes Alaska."

"He must, to stay here that long. For some people, it's a good place."

"He used to fish in these waters."

"Really? He seems to want to go back now. I can't say I blame him."

"Neither do I."

Major Barkison wondered if his own request to join a certain General in another theater would be granted. He hoped it would be. There were times when he felt his whole career was being blocked in this, now inactive, theater of war.

"Arunga's getting to be quite big, isn't it, Major?"

"Yes, it's about the best developed island here. Probably be quite a post-war base. Key to the northern defense."

"So I hear."

"Yes, the General was wise to build up Arunga."

"I hear he's got a big house there with a grand piano and all that sort of stuff."

Barkison laughed. "He lives in a shack."

"I guess somebody just started talking too much once." Martin looked about him. "I got to go up top now," he said. "Will you excuse me?"

"Certainly." Martin left through the galley.

Major Barkison sat down on a bench in the salon. He looked at the books in the rack. Most of them looked dull.

He sat quietly and studied the linoleum of the deck. The cracks in the linoleum formed interesting patterns, rather like lines on a battle map. He wondered just what battle these lines looked the most like. Probably Gettysburg. All maps looked like Gettysburg.

Bored, he examined the books again. One of them caught his eye: a book of short biographies. He picked it up and thumbed through the pages. The last biography was about General Chinese Gordon. Interested, he began to read. In his subconscious Wellington, for the time being, began to fade. A stage appeared in the mind of the Major, and he saw himself, the frustrated romantic, surrounded by Mandarins; dressed as General

Gordon, he was receiving a large gold medal for his defeat of the Wangs. Major Barkison could almost hear the offstage cheers of a crowd. He began to frame a speech of thanks in his mind. He could hear his own inner voice speaking brilliantly and at length of attrition. As Chinese Gordon he thought of these things.

ii

At ten o'clock, two hours after they had left the Big Harbor, Evans noticed that the barometer had dropped alarmingly.

He called Bervick over. Together they figured how much the barometer had fallen in the last two hours. Evans was worried; Bervick was not.

"I seen this sort of thing before," said Bervick. "Sometimes it's just the chain inside the barometer skipping a little, or maybe it's just for the time being. I seen this sort of thing before."

"Sure, so have I." Evans lowered his voice, he was afraid the man at the wheel might hear them. "I seen it blow all to hell, too, when the barometer dropped like this." Evans was nervous. He did not like to be nervous or seem nervous at sea, but lately some of the most trivial things upset him. A falling barometer, of course, was not trivial. On the other hand, it was not an unusual thing.

"Well, the weather don't look bad, Skipper. Take a look."

They opened one of the windows and looked out. The sky, though fog-ridden and dark, was no more alarming than ever. The sea was not high and the wind was light. The sea gulls were still hovering about the ship.

"I still don't like this," murmured Evans. "It's just the way it was the time the williwaw caught us off Umnak, remember that?"

"Sure, I remember. We been hit before. What you so hot and bothered about? You been sailing these waters a long time. We seen the barometer drop worse than this." Bervick looked at him curiously.

Evans turned away from the window. "I don't know," he said finally. "I just got the jumps, I guess. This weather gets under my skin sometimes."

"I know, it's no good, this crazy weather."

Evans took a long shaky breath. "Well, we're near enough to a lot of inlets if anything blows up."

"That's right."

"Tell the quartermaster to steer a half mile nearer shore."

"O.K." Bervick talked to the man at the wheel a moment. Evans looked at the chart of the islands. Bervick joined him and together they studied the chart and an old logbook which had been used on their last trip.

Evans rechecked the courses and the running times around the different capes. The stretches of open sea, while more vulnerable to the big winds, were generally safest. The capes and spits of rock were dangerous. One had to deal with them every fifteen minutes or so.

He checked the bays and inlets that they would pass. He also figured the times they would be abeam these openings. At the first sign of danger he would anchor inside one of these sheltered places. In the open sea they would have to weather any storm that hit them, but there would be no rocks in the open sea and that was a help.

"There's some good harbors on Kulak," said Bervick, examining that island on the chart.

"That's right, we'll be there early tomorrow morning. We'll leave this island around four in the afternoon. We'll coast along by Ilak for around six hours and then we hit open sea."

"It's about a hundred miles of open sea; it'll take us over nine hours. Then we reach Kulak."

"I'll feel O.K. there. Weather's good from there on."

"Sure the weather's always good from there on. It's always wonderful here." Bervick went back into his cabin. His watch did not begin until four.

Evans put away the charts. Then he stood by the window and watched the sky. Toward the southwest the clouds were dark, but the wind, which was faint, was from almost the opposite direction. The wind could change, though. When it was not strong and direct anything could happen.

Martin came into the wheelhouse. He looked at the barometer and whistled.

Evans was irritated. "Don't whistle in the wheelhouse. It's bad luck."

"You always do."

"That's different."

Martin chuckled, then, "Barometer's mighty low. How long she been dropping?"

"For almost two hours." Evans wished his first mate would not talk so loudly in front of the man on watch.

"That doesn't look . . ."

"No, it doesn't." Evans interrupted sharply. He looked warningly at the wheelsman. Martin understood. He walked over and stood beside Evans at the window.

"The sky looks all right."

"Sure. Sure. That's the way it always is."

"What's all the emotion for?"

"None of your damned business. Why don't you crawl in your sack?"

"I think I will." Grinning, Martin went into his cabin.

Gloomily Evans looked at the sky again. He knew that he must be acting strangely. He had never let them see him nervous before. Weather was beginning to get on his nerves after all his years in these waters.

The wheelhouse was getting a little warm, he noticed. He opened one of the windows and leaned out. The cold damp air was refreshing as it blew in his face.

* * * *

At eight bells Smitty announced lunch. Martin took Evans' place on watch. Bervick and Evans went below to the salon.

The passengers were already seated. Their morale, Evans could see, was quite high. Duval, oil streaks on his face and clothes, looked tired.

"Engines going smooth?" asked Evans sitting down.

"Just like always. Little bit of trouble with a valve on

the starboard, but that's all. The valve isn't hitting quite right."

"You got a spare part, haven't you?"

"Sure."

"Well, let's not worry."

Smitty brought them hash and coffee and crackers. He slammed the dishes down on the table.

"I feel as if I could eat a horse," said the Chaplain.

"You come to the right place," said Smitty. They laughed at the old joke.

"Any new developments?" asked the Major.

Evans shook his head. "No, nothing new. We're making about twelve knots an hour. That's nice time." He looked at Bervick. "Weather's fine," he added.

"Splendid," said the Major.

"What was that you were reading, Major, when we came in?" asked the Chaplain.

"A piece about General Gordon. A great tragedy, Khartoum, I mean. They were most incompetent. It's a very good example of politics in the army."

"Yes, I know what you mean," said O'Mahoney.

"Are there many seals in these waters?" asked Hodges.

Evans nodded. "A good many. If we see any salmon running you'll see a lot of seals chasing them. Sea lions hang around all the time."

"I saw some this morning," commented the Major. "I understand they're the fastest fish in the water."

"I believe they are classed as mammals," corrected the Chaplain, looking at Bervick who nodded.

"That's right, sir, they are mammals."

"You heard the Major," Duval suddenly said. "They are just big fish."

"A lot you know about fish," said Bervick coolly.

"I know enough about these things to know a fish when I see one swim in the water."

"Anybody with any kind of sense knows that sea lions aren't fish."

"So you're calling the Major and me dumb."

Bervick caught himself. "I'm sorry, Major, I didn't mean that, sir."

Major Barkison agreed, a little puzzled. "I'm sure

you're right, Sergeant. I know nothing about these things."

Bervick looked at the Chief triumphantly. He murmured, "That's like I said: they aren't fish."

The Chief was about to reply. Irritated, and a little worried that the Major might get the wrong impression of them, Evans said firmly, "I've heard all I want to hear about sea lions." Duval grumbled something and Bervick looked at his plate. The silence was awkward.

"When," asked the Chaplain helpfully, "do we get to Arunga?"

"It's about eight hundred miles. I always figure about seventy hours or more," Evans answered, glad to change the subject.

Evans thought of the falling barometer and the stormy sky. For some reason, as he thought, the word "avunculus" kept going through his head. He had no idea what it meant but he must have heard or read it somewhere. The desire to say the word was almost overpowering. Softly he muttered to himself, "avunculus."

"What was that?" asked Bervick who, sitting nearest him, had heard.

"Nothing, I was thinking, that's all."

"I thought you said something."

"What tonnage is this boat?" asked Hodges.

"Something over three hundred," answered Evans. He had forgotten, if he had ever known, the exact tonnage.

"That's pretty big."

"For a small ship it's average," said Evans. In the past he had sailed on all types of ships. He had been an oiler and a deckhand and finally master of a fishing boat outside Seward. Of all the ships he had been on, he liked this one the best. She was easy to handle. He would like to own a ship like this when the war was over. Many changes would have to be made, of course. The ship was so expensive to run that only the government could afford the upkeep. He could think of at least a dozen changes that should be made.

The others discussed the ship, and Duval told them about the engine room. He was proud of his engine room. Evans knew Duval was a fine engineer.

Evans looked at his empty plate and remembered that the hash had been good today. Smitty had put garlic in it and he liked garlic. The others seemed to like the hash, too, and he was glad. He always felt like a host aboard his ship. Ships were his home; this one in particular.

Before the others had finished, Evans motioned to Bervick and they excused themselves.

In the wheelhouse Evans took Martin's place on watch. There had been no change in the barometer.

"I want you to cut that stuff out," said Evans abruptly.

Bervick, who was playing with the dividers at the chart table, looked surprised. "Cut what out?"

"You know what I mean. All this arguing with the Chief. I don't like it and you better not let it happen again. You got more sense than to fight with him in front of some rank like the Major."

Bervick set his jaw. "No fault of mine if he wants to argue all the time. You tell him to keep out of my business and I won't say nothing."

"I'll talk to him, but you better remember too. I can't take much more of this stuff. You been at each other for months now."

"He gets in my hair. He gets in my business."

"For Christ's sake!" Evans exploded. "Can't you forget about that bitch? Can't you figure that there're a lot more where that one came from? What's wrong with you anyway?"

Bervick gestured. "I guess I just been up here too long. I guess that's what's the matter."

Evans was tired now. "Sure, that's it. That's what's wrong with all of us. We been to sea too long." Evans knew as well as Bervick the truth of this. After living too long in close quarters with the same fifteen or twenty men, one began to think and do irrational things. Women were scarce and perhaps it was normal that Bervick should feel so strongly. He watched Bervick as he fiddled with the dividers on the chart. He was a good man to have around. Evans liked his second mate.

"How's the barometer doing now?" asked Evans.

Bervick looked at it, twisting his hair as he did. "About the same. Bit lower, maybe."

Evans grunted. A mile ahead he could make out a long black spit of rock and stone and reef. As they approached it he changed the course. First five degrees to port, then ten, then they were around the point. The end of the island, some fifteen miles away, came clearly into view. This island was a big one and mountainous. In the clear but indirect light he could see the white peaks that marked the westernmost cape. Because of the size of the volcanic peaks the shore looked closer than it was.

"Sky's still dark," said Bervick. Evans noticed his mate's eyes were the color of the sea water. He had never noticed that before. It was an unusual thing, Evans thought, but having lived so long with Bervick he never really looked at him and probably could not have described him. Evans looked back at the sky.

"Still bad looking. I don't like it so much. Still we're keeping pretty close to shore. We can hide fast."

"Sure would delay us if something did blow up."

"It always does."

"You might," said Evans after a moment, "check the lifeboat equipment."

Bervick laughed. "We're being real safe, aren't we?"

Evans was about to say, "Better safe than sorry," but he decided that it sounded too neat. Instead he said, "You can't ever tell. They haven't been checked for a while."

"O.K., I'll take a look." He left through the door that opened onto the upper deck where the two lifeboats and one raft were kept.

Evans watched the dark long point they had just passed slowly fade into a harmless line on the water.

Martin returned from the galley. He glanced at the barometer as he came in. He did not comment on what he saw.

"What's the course?" he asked.

Evans told him.

"Where did Bervick go? Is he in the sack?"

"He's out on deck."

"He and the Chief were really going to town at lunch."

"Yeah, I don't like that stuff. I told Bervick to stop it."

"You better tell the Chief, too; a lot of this mess is his fault. You know the whole story, don't you?"

"Sure, I know the story. Bervick's been weeping over it long enough. I'm talking to the Chief, don't worry."

A gust of wet wind swept through the wheelhouse as Bervick came back in.

"Cold outside?" asked Evans.

Bervick shook his head. "Not bad. The boats are in good shape. Water's still fresh in the tanks."

"Good."

Bervick walked toward his cabin. "I think I'll turn in," he said.

"So will I." Evans wrote down the course and the time and a description of the weather in the logbook. "Get me up," he said to Martin, "if you see a ship or something. You got the course straight?"

"I got it."

Evans went into his cabin. He took the papers off his desk so that they would not fall on the deck if the ship should roll. He looked at himself in the mirror and said quite loudly, "Avunculus."

iii

Major Barkison found the Chief to be good, if not particularly intelligent, company. In the middle of the afternoon Duval had joined the Major in the salon. They talked of New Orleans.

"I have always felt," said the Major, recalling in his mind the French Quarter, "that there was no other place like New Orleans. It's not like New York. It is nothing like Paris." Major Barkison had never been to Paris but that was not really important.

"It sure is a fine place," said Duval. "Those women there are something." He winked largely at the Major who quickly agreed.

Duval continued, "Yes, I think of those women up

here all the time; anywhere, in fact, because there's just nothing like them anywhere."

"Yes," said the Major. He changed the subject. "Of course the food is wonderful down there; marvellous shrimp there."

"So do I like it. You know I used to know a girl down there who was pretty enough to be in the pictures, and she was some lay, too. I was just a young fellow at the time and she was maybe seventeen, eighteen then, and we sure played around together. She was sure some woman. I bet you can't guess what she's doing now?"

"No," said the Major, making a good mental guess. "No, I can't guess what she's doing."

"Well, she's got a big bar in New York and some girls on the side. I bet she makes more money than all of us put together. I got a picture of her here. I always carry her picture around with me. You can bet my wife don't like it." The Chief pulled a worn leather wallet from his pocket. He opened it and showed the Major a picture.

Major Barkison smiled stiffly and looked at the heavy mulatto nude. "Very nice," he said.

"You bet she is. She's some woman." He put away the wallet. "I'd sure like to see her again sometime. She is some woman."

"She seems to be," said the Major.

Duval looked into space. A distant expression came over his harsh and angular features. Barkison coughed. "Do you put into the Big Harbor often?" he asked.

Duval nodded, returning slowly to the present. "We stop in there once, twice a week. That's our regular run. It's the most civilized place on the Chain."

"Yes, I know. There seems to be an unusual number of civilians there. What's their status? I've never really looked into the problems of the civilian population up here, that's another department."

The Chief scratched himself thoughtfully. "Well, they're just here. That's all I know. They work in the stores. Some were pre-war residents. A lot of them are middle-aged women. We aren't supposed to have nothing to do with them. The army's real strict." The Chief laughed. "But there are all kinds of ways to operate. Them girls get pretty rich."

"I suppose they do. They seemed an awful-looking lot."

"Most of them are. There's one that isn't, though. She's Norwegian. You know the type, real blonde and clean-looking. She's real good. We been operating for some time now."

"Is that so?" The Major wondered how, as an up-holder of army regulations, he should take this. He decided he would forget it after a while.

"She's gotten around a lot, of course. You know the mate. The squarehead, Bervick."

The Major said he did.

"Well, him and this girl were hitting it off pretty well until I came along. So I give her some money and she's like all the rest and quits him. He acts like a big fool then. He hasn't caught on that she's the kind that'll carry on with any guy. He's dumb that way and I got no time for a damn fool."

"It seems a shame that you two shouldn't get along better."

"Oh, it's not bad. He just shoots off his mouth every now and then a little too much. He's a little crazy from being up here so long."

"I can imagine he might be. It's hard enough on shore with a lot of people. Must be a lot worse on a small ship."

Duval agreed. "It is," he said, "but you get used to it. When you get to be our age you don't give much of a damn about things. You do what you please, isn't that right, Major?"

Barkison nodded. He was somewhat irritated at being included in the same age group with the Chief. There was almost twenty years' difference in their ages. Major Barkison tried to look youthful, less like Wellington. He looked too old for thirty-one.

"Well, I think I'll go below and see if the engines are going to hold together." Duval gestured cheerily and walked out of the salon, balancing himself, catlike, on the rolling deck.

The Major got to his feet and stretched. He felt lazy

and at ease. This was the first real vacation he had had since the war began. It was good not to be writing and reading reports and making inspections.

He had enjoyed his visit to Andrefski Bay, though. The ATS Captain had been a bit hard to take but the officers had been most obliging. He had finally made out a report saying that the port should be closed except for a small housekeeping crew. This report had naturally made him popular with the bored men of Andrefski.

The Major walked about the empty salon, examining the books. They seemed as dull as ever to him. He decided he would finish reading about Gordon. He had read little more than a page when Hodges strolled into the salon and sat down beside him. The Major closed the book.

"A little rougher," commented Hodges.

"Yes. I suppose they've changed course again. Have you been up in the wheelhouse?"

"No, I was down in the focs'le. I was talking with some of the crew."

"Really?" Major Barkison was not sure if this was such a good thing; as experience, however, it might be rewarding. "What did they have to say?"

"Oh, not so much. They were talking about an Indian who drank some methyl alcohol the other night."

"Yes, I heard about that."

"Well, they were just talking. Same thing, or rather something very like it, happened to his brother down in Southeastern Alaska."

"Is that right?" The Major played with the book on his lap.

"He was working on a wharf on one of those rivers and he fell in. They said he never came up again. There was a lot of thick mud under the water and he just went down in it. People just disappear in it."

"Is that right?" The Major wondered if he would be sick again. The ship was beginning to roll almost as badly as it had on the trip to the Big Harbor.

"I guess that must be awful," said Hodges frowning, "to fall in the water like that and go right down. They said there were just a few bubbles and that was all.

Must have been an awful sensation, going down, I mean."

"I can imagine," said the Major. He remembered the time he had almost drowned in the ocean. His whole life had not passed in review through his head; he remembered that. The only thing he had thought of was getting out of the water. A lifeguard towed him in.

"You know they were telling me," said Hodges, "that there's an old Indian belief that if a dying man recognizes you, you will be the next to die."

"That's an interesting superstition. Did this fellow, the one who died last night, did he recognize anyone before he died?"

"No, as a matter of fact he was unconscious all the time."

"Oh."

Hodges tied one of his shoes thoughtfully. The Major could see he was still thinking of the Indian.

"What else did you hear?" asked the Major. He was always interested to know what the men thought of their officers. Sometimes their judgments were very shrewd.

"Not much, they talked a lot about Evans."

"Do they like him?"

"They wouldn't really say, of course; probably not, but they think he's a fine seaman."

"That's all that's really important."

"That's what I said. They say he married a girl in Seattle. He'd only known her a week."

"How long did they live together?"

"Around a month. He was up in Anchorage last month getting a divorce from her."

"Did she ask for it?"

"I don't guess they know. I gather he hadn't heard from her in the last three years."

"People should be more careful about these things," said the Major. He, himself, had been when he married the daughter of his commanding officer. She was a fine girl. Unfortunately her father had died soon after they were married. They had been happy, nevertheless.

Hodges got to his feet and said he thought he would go to the wheelhouse. He left. The Major put his book down on the floor. He was sleepy. There was something restful in the rocking motion of the ship. He yawned and stretched out on the bench.

* * * *

Major Barkison awoke with a start. The ship was pitching considerably. The salon was in darkness. Outside evening and dark clouds gave a twilight coloring to the sea and sky.

He looked at his watch. It was four-thirty. In the galley he could hear Smitty cursing among the clattering pots and pans. He turned on one of the lights in the salon. The salon looked even more dismal in the pale light.

He picked the book up from the deck and tried to read it, but the motion of the ship was too much for him.

Hodges came into the salon from the after door. His face and clothes were damp from spray; there was salt matted in his hair. His face was flushed.

"I've been out on deck, Major," he said, slamming the door shut. "She's really getting rough. The Skipper told me I'd better come back inside."

"Yes, it seems to be getting much rougher."

"I'll say." Hodges took off his wet parka and disappeared into the galley. A few minutes later he was back, his face and hair dry.

"What did Mr Evans have to say about the weather?"

"I don't know. He yelled to me out the window, that's all. I was on the front deck. So I came back in. The waves are really going over the deck."

"Oh." The Major was beginning to feel sick.

Chaplain O'Mahoney walked into the salon from the galley.

"Isn't this rolling dreadful?" he said. The Major noticed that the Chaplain was unusually pale.

"It's not so nice," said Major Barkison. O'Mahoney sat down abruptly. He was breathing noisily. "I certainly hope these waves don't get any larger," he said. He ran his hand shakily over his forehead.

"It couldn't be much of a storm," said the Major. "Mr Evans would have said something about it earlier. They can tell those things before they happen. There's a lot of warning." The Major was uneasy, though. Hodges, he noticed, seemed to enjoy this.

Major Barkison went to one of the portholes and looked out. They were in open sea now. The island was five or six miles behind them. Waves, gray and large, were billowing under the ship. On the distant shore he could see great sheets of white spray as the waves broke on the sharp rocks. A light drizzle misted the air.

Very little wind blew. The sky was dark over the island mountains behind them. No gulls flew overhead. A greenish light colored the air.

"What does it look like to you?" asked Hodges.

"Just bad weather, I guess. We're in the open now, I see."

"Yes, we left the island a little after four. We'll be near Ilak around seven tonight."

"I wonder which is best in a storm: to be near shore or out like this?"

Hodges shrugged, "Hard to tell. I like the idea of being near land. You don't suppose we're going to have one of those big storms, do you?"

"Heaven forbid!" said the Chaplain from his seat on the bench.

"Well, if it is one I have every confidence in the Master of the ship," said Major Barkison, upholding vested authority from force of habit. The idea of a storm did not appeal to him.

"I think we should go see Evans," said Hodges.

The Major considered a moment. "Might not be a bad idea. We should have some idea of what he plans to do. We might even go back to the Big Harbor."

"Let's go up, sir."

Hodges and the Major went into the galley. The Chaplain did not care to go. In the galley they found Smitty groaning in a corner. He was very sick.

They went up the companionway to the wheelhouse. Evans, Martin and Bervick were standing together around the chart table. Only Evans noticed them as they entered.

"Bad weather," Evans announced abruptly. "The wind's going to blow big soon."

"What's going to be done?" asked the Major.

"Wait till we've figured this out." Evans lowered his head over the chart. Together with his mates he talked in a low voice and measured distances.

Major Barkison looked out the windows and found the lurid view of sky and water terrifying. He wished that he had flown. He would have been in Arunga by now.

The Chief came into the wheelhouse. He spoke a moment with Evans who waved him away. Duval came over to the Major. "Bit of a storm," said Duval.

"Doesn't look good. You know about these things, does this look particularly bad to you?"

"I don't know. All storms are different. You don't know until it's over just how bad it was. That sky looks awful."

"Quite dark. This greenish light is new to me."

They watched the ink-dark center of the storm, spreading behind the white peaks of the island they had recently passed. Evans turned around and spoke to the Chief. "Engines in good shape?"

"That's right."

"Could you get up any more speed, say thirteen knots?"

"Not if you want to keep the starboard engine in one piece."

In a low voice Evans talked with Bervick. He spoke again to the Chief. "Keep going just as you are, then. Keep pretty constant. I'm heading for Ilak. The wind probably won't be bad until evening.

"If it holds off for a dozen hours or so, or if it isn't too strong, I'll take her into Kulak Bay tomorrow morning. We'll be safe in there." Evans spoke with authority. The Major could not help but admire his coolness. He seemed to lack all nervousness. The Major was only too conscious of his own nerves.

Hodges was listening, fascinated, his dark eyes bright with excitement. Major Barkison wished he could be as absorbed in events as young Hodges. I have too much imagination, thought the Major sadly. He would have to set an example, though. His rank and training demanded it.

"What would you like us to do, Mr Evans?" he asked.

"Keep cool. That's about all. Stay below and stay near the crew. If anything should go wrong, they'll get you in the lifeboats. The chances of this thing getting that bad are pretty slight, but we have to be ready."

"I see."

"Is the Chaplain in the salon?"

"Yes. I think he's sick. Your cook is, too."

"I can't help that. I'd appreciate it, Major, if you and the Lieutenant would go below. The mate who is not on duty here will stay in the salon with you. I'll have him keep you posted on what's happening."

"Right." Major Barkison was relieved to see Evans had such firm control of the situation. "We'll go down now," he said to Evans.

In the salon the Chaplain was waiting for them. "What did they have to say?" he asked.

"Going to blow pretty hard," the Major answered.

The Chaplain groaned. "I suppose we must bear this," he said at last in a tired voice. "These things will happen."

Duval walked in; he looked worried. "I don't like this so much," he said.

"It does seem messy," the Major answered, trying to sound flippant.

"Looks like the start of a williwaw. That's what I think it looks like. I could be wrong." Duval was gloomy.

"What," asked the Chaplain, "is a williwaw?"

"Big northern storm. Kind of hurricane with a lot of snow. Just plain undiluted hell. They come and go real quick, but they do a lot of damage."

"I hope you're wrong," the Major said fervently.

"So do I." Duval hurried off toward his engine room. Chaplain O'Mahoney sat quietly on the bench. Hodges watched the big waves through the porthole.

Major Barkison said, "I think I'll go to my cabin. If

anybody wants me, tell them I'm there. I'm going to try to sleep a little." This was bluff and he knew it sounded that way, but somehow he felt better saying it.

He opened the after door and stepped out on the stern. The ship was rocking violently and he had trouble keeping his footing. The wind was damp and cold. He waited for the ship to sink down between two waves, then, quickly, he ran along the deck toward the bow and his cabin.

A wall of gray water sprang up beside him, then in a moment it was gone and the ship was on the crest of a wave. He slipped on the sea-wet deck, but caught himself on the railing. As they sank down again into another sea-valley, he reached the door to his cabin. He went inside and slammed the door shut as spray splashed against it.

He stood for a moment in the wood-and-salt-smelling darkness. Great shudders shook him. Nerves, he thought. He switched on the light.

Water, he noticed, was trickling in through the porthole. He fastened it tight. More water was trickling under the door from the deck. He could do nothing about that.

Major Barkison took off his parka and lay down on his bunk. He was beginning to feel sick to his stomach. He hoped he would not become sick now.

If the ship went up on the crest of a wave within the count of three. . . .

Outside the wind started to blow, very lightly at first.

Chapter Four

i

BERVICK sat on a tall stool by the window, his legs braced against the bulkhead. The ship groaned and creaked as she was tossed from wave to hollow to wave again.

Evans stood near the wheelsman. He watched the compass. They were having trouble keeping on course, for with each large wave they were thrown several degrees off.

"Keep her even," said Evans.

"It's pretty hard. . . ." A wave crashed over their bow, spray flooded the windows for a moment. They were swung ten degrees to starboard.

"Hard to port," said Evans, holding tightly onto the railing.

The man whirled the wheel until they were again on course.

"Pretty hard, isn't it?" Bervick looked over at Evans.

"Not easy. Pitching like hell."

"Why not get her on electric steering?"

"Might break. Then where'd we be?"

"Right here."

Evans stood by the compass. He knew they could not afford to be even a few degrees off their course. Ilak was a small island, and if they should miss it. . . . Evans did not like to think of what might happen then.

He wished the storm would begin soon if it were going to begin at all. Waiting for the big wind was a strain, and there was no sign of the wind yet. Only the sea was becoming larger.

76

The sky was still dark where the heart of the storm was gathered. Dirty white snow clouds stretched bleakly in the damp almost windless air. The strange green light was starting to fade into the storm and evening darkness. Gray twenty-foot waves rolled smoothly under them, lifting them high and then dropping them down into deep troughs.

Evans noticed the man at the wheel was pale.

"What's the matter?" he asked. "You feeling the weather?"

"A little bit. I don't know why."

"You been drinking too much of that swill at the Big Harbor."

"I didn't have so much." The man spoke weakly. There were small drops of sweat on his forehead.

"You better get some air," said Evans. "I'll take her."

Quickly the man went to one of the wheelhouse windows, opened it, and leaned out. Evans took the wheel. He could get the feel of the ship when he was steering. He liked to take the wheel. Each time they descended into a trough they would be thrown several degrees off course. He would straighten them out as they reached the next wave-crest, then the same thing would happen again. It was not easy to keep the ship even.

"How's it feel?" Bervick asked.

"Fine. We're going to be knocked around a bit before we're through. May have to lash the wheel in place."

Spray splattered the windows of the wheelhouse. Salt water streamed down the glass making salt patterns as it went. Evans tried to make out land ahead of them, but the mist was too thick on the water. They were in the open sea now. Somehow Evans felt very alone, as though he were standing by himself in a big empty room. That was a favorite nightmare of his: the empty room. He would often dream that he had walked into this place expecting to find someone, but no one was ever there. Then he would dream that he was falling; after that he would wake up. Once in Anchorage a girl he had spent the night with told him that he had talked in his sleep. He told her his dream; she never dreamed, though, and could not understand.

Evans let his mind drift. Anything to keep from thinking of the coming storm. That was a bad thing about storms: you could not really get ready for one. Once you knew a storm was coming all you could do was wait and deal with it when it came.

He wondered what would be said if he lost the ship. He could hear the Captain at Andrefski saying, "I knew all along that guy Evans would crack up. I told him not to go." People were all alike that way. Make a mistake, or even have some bad luck and they'll say that they knew it was going to happen all along. People were all alike, thought Evans gloomily. He felt like a drink. He would not let himself have one, though. He would have to be able to think quickly. His stomach was already fluttering as he waited.

Evans looked over at the man on watch. He was still leaning out the window, his shoulders heaving. At last he turned around. He was pale but seemed relieved. "I guess I'm O.K. now," he said.

Evans stepped away from the wheel. "You sure you're not going to get sick again?"

"Yeah, I'm all right." The man took the wheel. Evans gave him the course. Then Evans walked to the port side where Bervick sat watching the water. He was daydreaming. His eyes were fixed on the sea.

In silence they looked out the windows. Except for an occasional sound of creaking from the bow, there was no sound to be heard in the ship. The wheelhouse was getting too warm, Evans thought. He unbuttoned his shirt. His hands shook a little as he did. This annoyed him.

"Getting warm, Skipper?"

"It's too hot in here. The Chief's really got the heat going fine. When we really need it in port he breaks something."

"Engine rooms are always like that. I'm glad I'm not an engineer."

The clock struck three bells. Evans looked at his watch. He always did that when the clock struck.

"When do you figure we'll be off Ilak?" Bervick asked.

"Just about two hours. Just about seven-thirty."

Bervick scratched his long hair thoughtfully. "I don't think this thing's going to blow up for a while."

"I don't either. We better just hope that we're near a good bay when it does. I expect we'll get the big wind tonight. It's taking a long time getting here."

"That's what I like." Bervick looked at the black unchanging storm center. "Maybe we'll miss the whole thing."

Evans smiled. "No chance, bucko, we'll get all of it. Right in the teeth, that's where we're going to get it."

"I wish I never left the Merchant Marine."

"You got a hard life."

"That's what I think."

"Don't we all." Evans made his mouth smile again. He tried to be casual.

His ex-wife would get his insurance, he thought suddenly. He remembered that he had not changed it from her name to his family's. He chuckled to himself. Everyone would be surprised. She would be surprised to get it; his family would be furious for not getting it. His father had four other sons and an unproductive farm. The insurance would be useful to them. He had not seen his family for seven years but sometimes they wrote to him. His mother always wrote. She was an educated woman but his father had never learned to read or write. He never felt there was much advantage in it. Evans thought of his family. His mind raced from person to person. He tried to recall how each of them looked. This was a good game that he often played with himself. It kept his mind off things that were bothering him, off storms, for instance.

Evans thought of his wife. She was a nice girl. If he had met her at any other time than during a war they might have been happy. He did not know her very well, though. He could not decide whether their marriage would have been any good or not. He wondered what she was doing now and where she was. He felt rather sad that he had not had time to know her better.

There were others, of course. There was consolation in that.

A wave, larger than the rest, hit violently across their bow. Evans staggered and almost fell. Bervick and his stool were upset and Bervick was thrown heavily on the deck. He stood up swearing.

"How did it feel?" asked Evans.

"Guess." Bervick limped across the wheelhouse and got the stool again. He placed it in one corner under the railing. He did not sit down again. "Waves getting larger," he said.

"We haven't seen nothing," said Evans. He looked at the compass. "Get on course," he said sharply. They were a dozen degrees off.

"O.K., O.K.," the wheelsman was beginning to sound a little desperate. He had not been at sea long.

Evans went back to his corner. He tried to recall what he had been thinking about, but his train of thought had been shattered. Only fragments were left to trouble him.

He looked at the forward deck. It had never looked so clean. The constant spray had made the gray-blue deck glisten. The door to the focs'le opened and a swarthy face appeared. The fat cook looked out at the slippery deck. Carefully the fat cook stepped up on the deck. A small wave hit the bow. He tried to get back in the focs'le but he was too slow. The wave threw him against the railing. Struggling, he was floating aft. Evans could see him, soaking wet, get to his feet at last and disappear in the direction of the galley.

"Some sailor, the cook," remarked Bervick.

"He's some cook, too. He can burn water."

The wheelhouse door opened and Martin joined them. His face showed no particular expression. He seemed to be unaware of the storm. He glanced at the barometer.

"A little lower," he remarked.

Evans looked at it, too. "Yes, the thing's fallen some more." He went to the chart table and recorded the barometer's reading in the logbook.

"When's the wind going to start?" Martin asked.

"Can't tell yet, John," Bervick said. "Around midnight, that's my guess."

"How're the passengers?" asked Evans.

"They're pretty bothered. The Chaplain's sick as a dog."

"Where'd the Major go when he left here?"

"He went to his cabin. I guess he's in the sack."

Evans frowned. "I wanted them to stay in the salon. You should have kept them there. Suppose he comes walking down the deck and a wave knocks him overboard?"

"That's an act of God," snapped Martin. For some reason Evans was pleased to have irritated his Mate. "Besides," Martin added, "he'd already gone when I went below."

"Well, when you go down again get him back in the salon. What's Hodges doing?"

"He thinks it's a game."

"I'm glad somebody's having a good time." Evans leaned against the bulkhead. The ship was not pitching quite so much now. The wind, what there was of it, was probably shifting. He remembered his insurance again. He wished he had taken care of it before they left. "Leave nothing undone and nothing begun," a Warrant Officer in Anchorage had told him. The words had a nice sound to them. They were also true.

"I've never been in a williwaw," remarked Martin.

Evans glanced at him. He did not like to hear a storm described aloud in advance. Evans had a complicated system of beliefs. If some things were mentioned before they happened they would take place exactly as mentioned. He never said much about bad weather before it broke. He would never have said this was going to be a williwaw. That was predicting, not guessing.

"Weren't you aboard that time we was off Umnak?" asked Bervick.

Martin shook his head. "I was having some teeth fixed. I missed that show."

"I guess you did at that. You'll make up for that now."

"I suppose I will."

A thirty-foot wave swept them amidships. The wheelhouse creaked as the salt water cascaded over them. Martin stumbled. The stool rolled across the deck. The man at the wheel lost his grip; the wheel spun around. Evans grabbed it quickly. His right arm felt as if it had been ripped off. With a great deal of trouble he got the ship on course again.

"You hang on this," he said to the wheelsman. "When you being relieved?"

"In a half-hour."

"Well, keep holding it tight. We don't want to wander all over this damned ocean."

"Pretty good-sized wave," said Bervick.

"Yeah, and there're more where that came from." Evans was breathing hard. The struggle with the wheel had tired him. His arm ached. He flexed it carefully.

"Get your arm?" Bervick was watching him.

"Just about pulled the thing off." Evans went to the window and leaned on the sill. The wave that had just hit them was a freak one, for the sea was not as high as it had been. The wind definitely seemed to be shifting. The sky was becoming darker. There was snow ahead.

Martin left them, and went below. Absently Evans rubbed his arm; it hurt him. He watched the water and waited for the big wind to come.

ii

Duval walked into the galley. He was hungry and, bad weather or not, he did not like to miss too many meals.

Several members of the crew were playing cards at the galley table. They were taking the storm casually. They pretended not to be interested in what was happening outside.

The ship rocked violently. Heavy coffee mugs slid back and forth on the galley table. Smitty sat in a corner of the galley, his chin on his knees. From time to time he would groan. The fat cook, in salt-soaked clothes, opened cans.

Duval took a can of hash out of the locker. The ship

rolled suddenly, slanting the deck. He stumbled across the galley and sat down on the bench with the others.

"Lousy, isn't it?" commented one of them.

"Just a little blow, that's all. You've never seen nothing till you've seen a tropical hurricane. This stuff up here is nothing like that. This is a breeze."

"Sure, we heard that one before, Chief."

"That's the truth." The Chief put food into his mouth. He had not realized how hungry he was. The fat cook poured him coffee.

The men talked about the Big Harbor and other things. They did not speak of the storm which was beginning. They spoke of the Indian who had died at the Big Harbor. Everyone told the story differently and Duval was bored to hear the story again. He had never liked Aleuts anyway. He looked at Smitty in the corner.

"What's the matter with you?" he asked.

"This water." Smitty cursed for several moments. "This the last trip I ever make. I seen everything now. I'm getting off this boat, I'm going back fast. We ain't never getting out of this." His dirt-colored hands gestured limply. The others laughed.

"Take it easy, Smitty," said the Chief. "You going to live forever." Smitty said nothing.

Duval chuckled. He was not frightened by bad weather. He had seen so many storms and he did have confidence in Evans. Duval was not worried.

The men talked of the Big Harbor and of all the things they had done.

"Say, Chief," said one, "did you see Olga?"

"Sure I saw her. I always see her. Anybody with money can see her."

The man laughed. "I guess Bervick isn't feeling so good today."

"He takes life too seriously," said the Chief and that was all he would say.

Hodges came into the galley from the salon.

"What've you been up to, Lieutenant?" asked Duval, genially.

"I've been wandering around the boat. I've never seen waves as big as they are outside. They must be over fifty feet."

"Not quite that big but they will be pretty soon."
Duval closed his eyes for a moment. He had found that
closing his eyes for a moment or so was very restful. It
soothed him to do this. He was not at all worried, of
course.

The light from the electric bulb overhead shone on
his eyelids, and he could see nothing but red with his
eyes shut, a warm clear red. He thought of the colorful
bayou land of Louisiana. Usually he did not care where
he was, but he did like color and there was no color
in the Aleutians, only light and shadow on rock and
water. The Chief opened his eyes.

Hodges was biting his thumbnail. The Chief watched
him. He wondered what he might have done if he had
been as well educated as Hodges. Probably the same
things. Life was about the same for all people; only
the details varied.

"I hear they expect the big wind around midnight,"
said Hodges.

"That's what Evans says. He don't know, though. He
guesses just like the rest of us do. We guess, we all
guess and most of the time we're wrong." The Chief
enjoyed discrediting Evans occasionally.

"Well, it should be some sight. I'm glad I'll be able
to see it." One of the deckhands laughed.

"You won't like it so much," said Duval. "Even
though these blows up here aren't nothing compared to
what we used to have in the Gulf." The crew laughed.
Anything that could keep their minds away from the
coming storm was good.

"What's happened to the Chaplain?" asked Duval.

"He's in the salon. I expect he's feeling bad. He
doesn't take to this sea business at all."

"I suppose I'd better go see how he is." Carefully
Duval got to his feet and walked across the deck. He
slipped once and swore to himself as he did. His balance wasn't as steady as it had once been.

Chaplain O'Mahoney was sitting at the galley table,
his jaw set and his face white. He was playing solitaire.
He looked up as they came in and he managed to
smile.

"I suppose it will be worse," he said.

Duval nodded.

"That's what I expected."

"This'll really be something to tell our grandchildren," said Hodges cheerfully. The Chaplain laughed.

"Something to tell *your* grandchildren," he said.

"If you ever live to have any," remarked Duval.

They sat together around the table, each thinking of the storm. Duval watched the Chaplain's hands. They were white and plump and helpless. The Chaplain, Duval thought, could not have fixed a valve or even changed a sparkplug in a car. Of course the Chaplain knew many things. He could speak Latin, and Duval was impressed by Latin and the Church rituals. O'Mahoney's soft hands could give blessings and that was an important thing. Perhaps it made no difference that his hands were not practical.

"Are you Catholic?" asked O'Mahoney, turning to Hodges.

The Lieutenant shook his head. "No, we're Episcopal down home."

"Indeed? I have known some very fine Episcopal ministers, very fine ones."

"We've got a lot of them down home, ministers I mean."

"I should suppose so. I knew some before I went into the monastery."

"What's a monastery like, sir?"

"Just like anything like that would be. Just the way you'd expect it to be. Perhaps a little like the army."

"It must be queer, being so out of things."

"One's not so far out of the world. There is certainly nothing harder than living in close quarters with a group of people."

"I thought it was supposed to be a kind of escape."

"Certainly not. We have more time to think about the world. Of course, we do own nothing, and that makes life much simpler. Most people spend all their lives thinking of possessions."

"I suppose you're right," said Hodges. Duval did not listen as they talked. Instead he walked restlessly about the salon.

Through the after door he watched the white wake

foaming. The wind appeared confused: blowing from first one direction and then shifting to another. There was snow in the clouds overhead.

The ship was tossed about like a stick in a river current. But somehow they managed to keep on course. The Chief tried not to think of this. He thought instead of a gauge on the starboard engine, but even that was too close to the storm. He turned and went back to the Chaplain and Hodges. Religious talk was soothing if nothing else.

He asked O'Mahoney about his monastery. O'Mahoney was happy to talk of it.

"A very simple place. There's really not much to tell. We all have our different jobs."

"What sort of work did you do?" asked Hodges.

"Well, I was in charge of the novices. Those are the beginners, the apprentices."

"Sounds like a First Sergeant's job," said Hodges.

"Very much the same. I wish," said the Chaplain wistfully, "that I was back in Maryland now."

"So do I," agreed Duval. "In New Orleans, I mean. I'm tired of this place."

"We all are, but here we are. You have a wife, I suppose, in New Orleans?"

"Yes, I got a wife and two kids. We lost a new one two years ago. I guess she was too old to be having kids."

"Such a pity, your child dying."

"One of those things, they happen all the time. I saw the kid only once so it wasn't so bad."

The Chief sat down beside the Chaplain. Duval reached in his pocket and took out a knife. Carefully he whittled his fingernails. He concentrated on what he was doing. He would think of nothing else for a while.

Suddenly the ship lurched and Duval was thrown off the bench. His knife clattered on the deck.

He got to his feet quickly. The Chaplain was holding onto the bench with both hands, his face very white. Hodges was braced against a table. Duval looked down at his hand, conscious of a sharp pain: he had cut one of his fingers and it was bleeding. He waved his hand in the air to cool away the pain. Bright red blood in a thin stream trickled down his hand. The waving did not help. He stuck his finger in his mouth.

"You'd better get a bandage on that," said O'Mahoney helpfully.

"Yes," agreed Hodges. "That's dangerous, cutting yourself."

"I know, I'll fix it. You people better hang around here until Evans decides what to do. You might get the Major up." Holding his finger in the air, Duval went quickly down the companionway and into his engine room.

His two assistants were sitting beside the engines. They wore dirty dungarees and thin shirts; it was hot in the engine room. One of the oilers crouched in a corner. He had come aboard only the week before. Fumes from the oil, as well as the motion of the ship, had made him sick.

The two assistants, however, had been in this engine room in all sorts of weather for several years. They sat now under the bright electric lights and read muchhandled magazines about Hollywood.

The Chief went aft to his stateroom in the stern. Carefully he wrapped a piece of gauze about his finger and then he tied the ends of the gauze into a neat bow. When he had finished he sat down on his bunk. He had always hated the sight of blood. He closed his eyes and took a deep and shaky breath. His heart was pounding furiously.

The first assistant came into the cabin.

"What's the matter, Chief?"

"Not a thing." Duval sat up straight and opened his eyes. "Cut my finger, that's all. How's that starboard engine sounding?"

"She sounds O.K., she's going to be O.K." The man leaned against the bulkhead. He was stout and redheaded and a good mechanic. He came from Seattle.

"Say, what's this I hear that there's going to be a big wind soon? Is that right?"

"I expect so. Evans don't seem so bothered but the barometer's gone down low. Going to have a williwaw."

"It must be blowing hard outside. We been feeling it rock pretty bad but that's not new on this run. Maybe I ought to go up and take a look." The assistants seldom left the engine room. Several times they had gone through bad storms and had not known it until later. Even violent pitching and tossing did not alarm them.

"The wind ain't too bad yet. Blowing maybe sixty, maybe more. It's not coming from anywhere certain yet. The sea's big, though."

"Think we'll anchor somewhere?"

"I don't know. That guy Evans never tells us anything and I'm sure not going to ask him anything. Yes, I guess we'll anchor in Ilak."

"Well, it won't be the first time we had to anchor in like that."

"No, it won't be the first time."

Duval fingered the blue and white bedspread his wife had made for him and, fingering it, he thought of Olga. He hoped they would spend more time in the Big Harbor on the trip back.

"What did you do last night?" he asked.

His first assistant shrugged. "I didn't do so much. Got tight, that's all."

"Too bad. Did you see that squarehead Bervick last night?"

"I saw him for a little while. He was in the Anchorage Inn. He was with old Angela. She's sure a fat woman."

Duval chuckled. "Serves him right. He was trying to sew up Olga. He wasn't so smart about it. She'd come running if he didn't keep bothering her about the others she sees. After all she's got to make some money, like everybody else."

"I heard that one before." His assistant laughed. "She's a fair looking girl, Olga is."

"She certainly is." Duval looked at his finger. He examined the bandage closely to see if the blood was seeping through. He was relieved to see it was not. "Let's take a look around," he said.

"O.K., Chief."

They went back to the engine room. The other assistant was reading his magazine. He sat, teetering his chair with each lunge of the ship. Duval walked between the engines, checking the gauges and listening for trouble. Everything appeared in order. He switched on the hold pumps. When they were in a big sea the hold leaked badly; there was a leak somewhere but no one had ever found it.

Duval was pleased. If anything should happen to the ship now it would be Evans' fault. The Chief did not like to take the blame for anything and in that he was quite normal.

He glanced at the oiler in the corner. For a moment he wondered if he should get him some ammonia or something because he looked so ill. He decided not to; when you were seasick you liked to be alone.

"Everything looks fine," he said to his assistants. Then he went aft again to his stateroom, carefully examining his bandage for signs of fresh blood.

iii

The night was dark. Off the port side Martin could barely make out the coastline of Ilak. Since seven-thirty they had been searching for the place where Evans intended to anchor.

Martin stood close to the window. He could hear waves crashing loudly on the near-by shore. The wind was increasing and the sea was becoming larger. He held tightly to the railing, his stomach fell dizzily as they sank into an unusually deep trough.

Evans had taken the wheel himself and the man on watch stood beside him ready to help in case the wheel should get out of control. Bervick stood by the chart table. From time to time he would call out their position.

The wheelhouse was dark except for dimmed lights in the binnacle and over the chart table. Martin could hear the wind howling around the corners of the wheelhouse. It sounded seventy or eighty miles an hour, and this, according to Evans, was just the start.

Martin made a quick dash for the chart table.

"When'll we get there?" he asked.

Bervick did not look up. "Ten minutes and we should be abeam."

"What's that?" Evans asked, his voice pitched high above the wind.

"We're getting close, that's all. That inlet you're looking for. Two miles away, as I figure."

"Good." Evans motioned to the man on watch who quickly took the wheel. Then Evans opened a window on the port side. A tremendous roar of wind and breaking water exploded into the wheelhouse. Spray splattered in Evans' face as he watched the coastline.

Martin and Bervick went over and stood near him. Less than a mile ahead Martin could see a long spit of high rock pointing out into the sea. "That it?" he asked.

Bervick nodded. "Just around the corner there. Nice deep bay."

"All right," said Evans, speaking to the man at the wheel. "Bring her to port, five degrees. Ring Stand By, Mate."

Martin skidded across the deck. He rang the engine room several times on the telegraph. Then he set the markers on Stand By.

They waited for the Chief to answer. Two minutes passed and then the Chief rang back. He was ready.

"Half Speed Ahead," said Evans.

Martin set the markers on Half Speed. The ship's vibration changed. Waves which had once crashed against them now lifted the ship easily onto their crests.

Evans turned to Martin.

"Go below and get some of the crew. Be ready to anchor when I give the word. When we get out of the wind you and your men go out on the forward deck and stand by."

"Right." Martin went quickly below. The idea of going out on deck in this weather did not appeal to him. Someone had to do it, though.

He gathered two deckhands in the galley. They cursed loudly but he knew they were glad to be anchoring.

Then, the ship having rounded the point, they went outside on the forward deck. Martin was almost thrown off his feet by a gust of wind. Though somewhat protected by the hills, they were not yet completely out of the storm. The wind was cold and penetrating. It chilled him, even through his heavy parka. Water whipped their faces. The deck was dangerously slick and the ship still pitched badly. On hands and knees, their eyes barely open and smarting from the salt, they wormed their way forward to the bow and the anchor winches.

They reached the bow. Martin got to his feet, holding tightly onto the tarpaulin which covered the winch. The other two did the same. Luckily they knew their job so well that he would not have to make himself heard over the sea-thunder.

The deckhands swiftly slipped the tarpaulin off the winch. Martin stood beside the lever which operated the anchor. The other two stood ready to knock the brakes from the chain.

He watched as the ship skirted the teethlike rocks and headed into a small bay. Dark mountains stood large against the sky. The bay itself was less than a mile wide and perhaps a little more than a mile deep. Mountains rimmed it on three sides.

Abruptly the ship stopped pitching. They were out of the wind at last. Inside this bay there was neither wind nor a large sea.

Evans leaned out of the wheelhouse window and waved.

"Let her go," said Martin.

There was a loud clanging and then the metallic sound of falling chain as the freed anchor dropped into the water. The ship drifted slowly. Evans had stopped the engines.

Patiently Martin waited for the tug which would tell them the anchor was secured in the sea-floor. The ship glided ahead softly, cutting the small waves as it moved shoreward: a slight jolt and the ship stopped; rocking slightly, she began to circle about.

"Anchor's holding," shouted Martin. Evans waved and shut the wheelhouse window. Martin and the deckhands went back to the galley.

Martin stood before the galley range and tried to warm himself. Water had seeped through his shirt to his skin and he was completely wet. He could not remember when he had been so cold. The two men who had been out on deck with him were also shivering.

He slipped off his parka and shirt and then he rubbed himself in front of the stove. His teeth chattered as he began to get warm again.

"Going to be here long, Mate?" asked one of the men.

"We'll probably leave at dawn. Wind should let up then."

"Getting better then?"

"Yes," said Martin, knowing it was not getting better. "Storm should be over by morning."

"That's good." The men talked a while longer. Then they went to the focs'le. In his corner Smitty began to stir. Groaning, he got to his feet and walked over to the range and poured himself some coffee.

"You feel bad?" Martin asked.

"You bet I feel bad." Smitty walked unsteadily away.

Martin sat down for a moment. He was tired, more tired than usual. Lately it seemed that he was always tired. He wondered if something was wrong with him. Perhaps he should see a doctor and get sent back to the States.

Everything was quiet, he noticed gratefully. It seemed that there had been nothing but noise since they left the Big Harbor that morning.

"Say, Martin." He turned around and saw Evans standing in the door. "Come on out and help me nest the boom. Somebody didn't do a very good job when we left." This remark was meant for him and if he had not been so weary he would have snapped back; the effort, however, was too great.

"Sure, sure," Martin said.

On the forward deck the wind was direct but not strong. Small waves slapped the sides of the ship. The hills seemed peaceful and only a faraway roar reminded them of the storm.

They stood beside the mast, Evans absently twisting a wet rope. "I'll go up top," he said finally. "You let the boom down." He walked away. A few moments later Evans appeared on top of the wheelhouse.

"Let her down easy," he shouted.

Martin let the boom descend slowly into place. He had to admire the quickness with which Evans lashed the mast secure.

"O.K.," said Evans and he disappeared.

Bemused by the quiet, Martin walked back to the stern. He stood a while watching the mountains. He noticed that the side of one sharp peak seemed oddly blurred. It was the snow being ripped off the mountains by the wind. In the daylight it was a wonderful sight.

He walked slowly into the salon. His watch started at midnight. He would sleep on one of the salon benches until then. He was tired.

* * * *

A few minutes after twelve Martin was awakened by Evans.

"Your watch," said Evans. "I'm going to get some sleep. If anything looks bad, get me up."

"Sea still high outside?"

Evans nodded. His eyes looked sunken, Martin noticed, and his lids were red.

"We'll leave around sunup if we do leave, that right?"

"That's right," said Evans. "We'll leave in the morning."

They went up to the wheelhouse. Evans went to his cabin. Martin and the men on watch stood silently in the pale light of the wheelhouse. They listened to the sea.

"Think the radio will work, Mate?"

"We can find out." Martin turned the radio on. A blast of static thundered out at them. "I guess not," said Martin and he turned it off.

He noticed the barometer was still low. He recorded the time and the barometer reading in the logbook.

"I'm going below for a while," he said.

Outside on deck there was little wind and the dark night was serene. He glanced at the higher mountains; the wind was still violent, for snow was blurring the peaks. He went toward the bow and down into the focs'le.

It was warm inside the focs'le and the lights were

burning brightly. Bunks in two tiers lined the bulk-heads. Some of the men were sleeping; others sat on their bunks and talked. In the middle of the deck the ship's dog was licking a bone.

The men who were awake looked up as Martin came down the ladder.

"How's it going, Mate?"

"Fine. The bulkheads sweating much?"

"I'll say they are." The man who spoke brushed his hand over the wood. "Look," he said. Beads of water clung to his fingers.

"That's pretty lousy," said Martin. "At least it's not cold in here."

"Well, if it was we'd all be dead. This is the dampest boat I was ever on." The others agreed. Martin sat down on an empty bunk and looked around. The focs'le was even sloppier than normal. It was, of course, bad most of the time and nothing could be done about it. Evans had tried to do something with no success. He had only made himself unpopular with the men.

Clothes littered the deck and the bunks were un-made. Old shoes and much-gnawed bones had been hidden in the corners by the dog. Martin could see why Evans hated dogs, especially on ships.

None of these things were important now, though. Nothing, except getting out of the storm, was impor-tant.

"I wonder how she's blowing outside?" remarked a deckhand.

"Ought to be hitting a hundred about now," an-swered another. "What do you think, Mate?"

"I hope it's a hundred. If it is that means the storm'll be over by morning. They don't last so long, these storms."

"That's what I say."

The men spoke together in low voices. Martin ex-amined the pin-up pictures that plastered the bulk-heads. Whenever he thought of his army career he thought of these pictures first. Somehow they almost never changed no matter where he was. These pictures and the radio, those were the two constant things. Oc-casionally there was no radio but the pictures were always there: half-dressed girls, in mysteriously lighted bedclothes, promising sex.

He thought of the three years he had spent in the army, and, of those years, only a few things stood out in his memory: certain songs that were popular when he had left for overseas, the waiting in line for almost everything. . . . The rest of his army career came to him only as a half-feeling of discomfort.

The dog, he noticed, was chewing his shoe. He grabbed the animal by the muzzle and pushed it away.

He got up. "See you," he remarked at large and he began to climb the ladder that led to the forward deck.

"See you, Mate."

Major Barkison sat at a table in the salon, a stack of writing paper in front of him.

"Good evening, sir," said Martin.

"Good evening. Things seem a bit quieter now."

"Yes, we'll be able to get some sleep."

"I'm glad to hear that. I never thought the sea could get so rough." The Major contemplated the fountain pen in his hand. "I was," he confided, "quite sick."

"I'm sorry. You should have let us know, we've got some stuff to take care of that."

"Have you really? I felt so terrible that I couldn't get out of my bunk. I've never seen such jumping around. Does this sort of thing happen often?"

"Not too often, thank God."

"It was quite enough." The Major stroked his bald brow. The veins stood out on his hand. Martin hoped the Major had nothing seriously wrong with him. It was one of Martin's nightmares that someone should have appendicitis or something like that aboard ship when they would be unable to help. Such things had happened before on other ships.

"I've been doing a little letter writing," the Major explained, pointing to the papers. "I can really get caught up on a trip like this."

"Would you like some coffee, Major?"

"Why yes, very much."

Martin went into the galley and poured two cups from the pot which always sat, warming, on the stove.

He brought the cups back into the salon and set them down on the table.

The Major grunted his thanks. They drank the dark and bitter liquid. Martin warmed his hands on the coffee mug. His hands were cold and stiff from climbing the focs'le ladder without gloves.

"Tell me, Mr Martin," said the Major finally, "do you feel . . . I know it's a tactless question, in fact an unethical question to ask . . . but do you feel that Mr Evans is . . . well, quite capable of handling this situation?"

Martin smiled to himself. "Yes, Major. I have a lot of faith in Evans; when it comes to sailoring he's one of the best seamen up here."

"I'm very glad to hear you say that. I should never have asked, of course. But the situation being as it is, well, I thought it best to get your opinion."

"I quite understand."

"I hope you'll regard my question as confidential, Mr Martin."

"I certainly shall."

"Thank you." The Major sighed and sketched cartoons of sinking ships on a piece of paper.

"The Chaplain gone to bed?" asked Martin.

"I expect so. I haven't seen him for several hours."

"It looks like the old jinx is at work again."

"What do you mean?"

"Well, every time we carry a Chaplain we have a bad storm."

"O'Mahoney must be a potential Bishop if one goes by results," commented the Major.

Martin laughed. "He's done pretty well so far."

The Major played with his pen a moment. "Where," asked Martin, "do you expect to be stationed after the war, sir?"

"Well, I should like Tacoma, naturally, but I think I'll be sent to Washington, D.C. A tour of duty there is worth more than a lifetime of field work."

"I've always heard that."

"It is not," said the Major wisely, "what you know, it is who you know."

"You certainly are right."

"Yes, that's the way it is." They pondered this great truth in silence. Martin finally got to his feet.

"I hope you'll feel better tomorrow, Major. We'll leave in the morning; it should be calm by then."

"I hope so, good night."

"Good night." Martin walked slowly through the galley. The lights were still on. He snapped them off. Then he walked out on deck.

A pleasant breeze cooled his face. Water lapped quietly against the sides of the ship. The night sky was black. In another forty-eight hours, if all went well, they would be in Arunga.

As he stood there many dramatic speeches came to Martin. Plays he had read or had seen on the stage came to him. The rolling periods of the Elizabethans flowed through him like water in a rock channel. He always enjoyed these moments when he could think of words and voices speaking words.

He walked about on the deck. He stood by the railing on the port side and breathed the clean air. In these islands there was no odor of earth and vegetation in the wind, only the scent of salt and stone. He raised his head and looked at the mountains. The snow still whirled seaward.

Chapter Five

i

MORNING.

Evans walked into the wheelhouse. He had slept unusually well. As a rule he stayed awake during bad
weather, but this time he had really slept and he was
glad that he had.

Bervick, whose watch it was, stood looking at the
barometer.

"What do you think, Skipper?"

Evans looked at the barometer: still low, there had
been almost no change overnight.

"I think there must be something wrong with the
thing. You seen them act up before, haven't you?"

Bervick agreed. "They can be wrong. It looks fine
outside." Evans went over to the window. There was
little light in the sky, but the pre-sunrise stillness was
good. Even in the mountains there was no wind.

"What do you think, Skipper?"

"I don't know. I'll have to think about it. I don't
know." Evans felt suddenly inadequate. He wished that
he did not have to make this decision. He wondered
for a moment what would happen if he got into his
bunk and refused to get out. When he was very young
he had often had a feeling like that: to lie down somewhere and not move and let unpleasant things take
care of themselves.

"I suppose," he said finally, "seeing as how the wind
has died down, I suppose we should take a chance."

"We'll make a dash for Kulak if anything goes
wrong."

Evans went to the chart table. Mentally he computed distances and positions. "We'll take a chance," he repeated. "Get Martin up."

Bervick went into his cabin; he came out, a moment later, with Martin.

"Bervick," said Evans, "you take some men out on deck and get ready to weigh anchor. Martin, you go on down and see how the passengers are doing. Talk to the Chief and tell him we're leaving right away. We want to get to Arunga tomorrow night."

Martin and Bervick left together. Evans looked at the compass; he looked at the barometer, and then he looked at the chart. He walked out on deck and watched morning move slowly into the east. The day looked peaceful; there was no way, though, to tell what might happen. There never was any way to tell.

He watched Bervick and several deckhands as they walked on the forward deck, testing the winches, preparing to weigh anchor. Evans went to the telegraph and rang the engine room. He set the markers on Stand By. Almost immediately the Chief rang back.

Evans took a deep breath. Then he opened the window and yelled, "Pull her up!"

Bervick pushed a lever. There was much clanging and rattling. The anchor chain came up easily. Evans let the ship drift slowly with the tide. At last, satisfied that the anchor was free, he gave the engine room Slow Speed Astern.

The ship, vibrating strongly, drew away from shore. Evans twirled the electrical steering gear hard to starboard and headed the ship for the opening and the sea beyond.

At Slow Speed Ahead they moved through the channel, neatly cutting the still water. The uneven rocks of the point moved by them. A raven, the first he had seen since they left Andrefski, flew warily among the rocks. A damp breeze came to him through the window. Snow clouds hung over the mountains.

Bervick came back. "All squared away. We left the tarpaulin off. Just in case we might need the anchor again."

"Good." Evans motioned to the man on watch who had been standing by the door. "You take over."

Evans examined the blue-green paint of the wheelhouse. It was too dark. He had thought so when they first used it, but this dark color was the only paint he could get. A lighter color would have been much better. He would have everything repainted when they got back to Andrefski.

Without warning the ship was lifted several feet in the air by a long wave. They were out of the inlet. The rocks of the point receded in the distance.

"Bring her to port," commanded Evans. The bow swung parallel to shore. They were headed west again.

"So far so good," said Bervick.

Evans agreed. There was quietness in the morning. There would be snow flurries but the big wind seemed to have gone. Evans was glad. He began to whistle.

Bervick looked at him. "We're not in the clear yet," he said.

Evans laughed, "I guess you're right. I just feel good. I wish I knew what was the matter with that damned barometer, though."

"Maybe that little chain's stuck, like I said."

"Might be."

Martin joined them. "The passengers look fine today," he said.

"The Chief say everything's working in his department?"

"That's what he said. Smitty's got breakfast ready. They're eating now."

Evans remembered that he had had nothing to eat for almost a day. "I think I'll go below," he said.

"O.K., Skipper." Bervick went over to the chart table and Martin went into his cabin.

The galley, Evans saw, was much more cheerful today. Smitty had cleaned the deck and straightened the unbroken china. Several deckhands sat at the galley table talking loudly. You could tell, thought Evans, how long a man had been up here by the way he talked. The longer a man was in the islands the longer his stories were. Talking was the only thing to do when there was no liquor.

The passengers were eating heartily.

"Good morning," said Evans, entering the salon.

"Good morning," said the Chaplain, giving the phrase its full meaning. "There is practically no rocking," he observed happily.

"This may be a quiet trip yet," said Evans. He sat down and Smitty brought him breakfast. The Major was in a good mood. He was not even pale today, Evans noticed.

"I hear we may be in Arunga tomorrow night," said the Major.

"That's what we hope," said Evans. Breakfast tasted better than it ever had before.

"I shall really be glad when this trip is over," said the Chaplain. "Not of course that I haven't every confidence. . . . But, you know, I just wasn't designed for ocean-going. You don't think it will rock much, do you?"

Evans shook his head. "I don't think so."

Duval and his assistants arrived and sat down at their end of the table.

"Didn't blow up after all, did it, Skipper?" said Duval.

"We're not there yet." Evans could not resist saying this. Duval liked to be positive. Especially about things which were none of his business.

"Well, it looks to me like clear sailing." Duval spoke flatly. He stirred his coffee.

"How fast are we going?" asked Hodges suddenly.

"Nine, maybe ten knots," Evans answered.

"Nearer twelve, I'd say," commented the Chief.

"Engineers are all the same," said Evans. The Chief said nothing.

"You people should be going home shortly," Major Barkison announced. Evans looked up and the others were interested, too.

"Yes," the Major continued, "we're going to close down Andrefski, as you've probably gathered. That's why I was out there. When it closes down those of you who are due for rotation will probably get it. We don't need any more sailors here."

"That's good news," said Evans thoughtfully. The

Chief and his assistants questioned the Major further and Evans thought of Seattle. He would get married again. That would be the first thing he would do. After that he would get a second mate's berth on some liner. He would come back to these islands again. Someday, perhaps, he might get a fishing boat and live in Seward. There were many things that he would do.

"If you'll excuse me," said the Major, rising, "I think I'll write some more letters." The other passengers also left the table.

"Martin tells me," said Duval, "that the barometer's still low. What do you think's wrong?"

Evans shrugged. "I don't know. We'll have to wait and see what happens."

"We were going to do that anyway," said the Chief sourly and he left the table, his assistants close behind.

Evans wondered why he had so much trouble getting along with his crews. When he had been a second mate on a cargo ship he had had no trouble, in fact he had even been popular. Somehow things just didn't work as easily aboard this ship. He wondered if he might not be too much of a perfectionist. People didn't like to live with that sort of thing. He spun his coffee mug between his hands. Finally he stood up. "Smitty," he said loudly. "You can clear the table now."

Bervick had the case off the barometer, when Evans returned to the wheelhouse. Bervick and Martin were examining the mechanism.

"Find anything wrong?" asked Evans.

Bervick shook his head. "There's nothing wrong with it. The thing's in good order." Evans frowned. He did not like to think of what would happen if this reading were correct. He went to the chart table.

They would be off Kulak around one o'clock in the afternoon. Between his present position and Kulak there was open sea and no protection. He felt suddenly sick. Without a word to the others he walked out on deck.

The air was cool and moist. There was no wind and no sign of wind. Dark clouds hung motionless in the air. He felt the vastness of this sea and the loneliness of one small boat on the dividing line between gray sky and gray water. They were quite alone out here and he was the only one who realized it. This was very sad, and feeling sad and lonely he went back into the wheelhouse.

Martin and Bervick had gone below, he was told by the man at the wheel.

Evans stood by the window on the port side and watched Ilak disappear. Snow, coming from the west, he noticed, was bringing wind with it. He closed the windows.

Martin returned silently. He looked at the snow clouds. "We won't be able to see so well," he said.

Evans nodded. "We got the times figured out pretty well. I don't like coming so near to Kulak, sailing blind."

They waited then for the snow to start.

At a few minutes to nine whiteness flooded them. Snow splattered softly on the window glass. Luckily there was enough wind to keep it from collecting on the windows. Below them Evans could see the deck being covered with snow. The sea had increased in size but was not yet large.

Bervick joined them.

"Just a little snow," said Evans.

"That's the way a lot of them start."

"A lot of what?"

"Williwaws."

"Sometimes, maybe." Evans thought of the low barometer.

"Remember that one off Umnak?" asked Bervick.

"Sure, I remember it."

"That one started this way."

"Not with snow. It started with a little wind."

"A little wind like this and a lot of snow. You remember the snow, don't you?"

"Yes, I guess I forgot about it. That was a year ago."

"That was a lousy thing."

"We got out of it fine." Evans' hands were cold and his stomach kept being flooded with something.

"Sure, we got out of it. Our luck should hold." Bervick sounded cheerful.

"It had better," said Evans and he blew on his hands to warm them.

ii

"Not much change," said Martin. Evans had been in the engine room with Duval since lunch. It was two o'clock now and snow still swept over the water.

Evans looked gloomily at the whiteness. Martin watched him closely to see what his reactions were. Evans only frowned.

To the south the snow flurries were thinning a little and they could see the dark outline of Kulak. They had been abeam the island for over an hour.

"Kulak," remarked Evans.

"We've been in sight of it since one."

"A lot of good harbors there," said Evans.

"Thinking of anchoring, maybe?"

"I'm always thinking of anchoring." Evans walked over to the compass and watched it.

Martin yawned. The monotony of waiting was beginning to get on his nerves.

Evans walked slowly about the wheelhouse. "That wind's a lot stronger outside," he said suddenly.

Martin was surprised. "I don't think so. I think you're wrong."

"Don't tell me I'm wrong," Evans flared. Martin said nothing; he had seen Evans upset before. Sometimes he acted oddly. "Weather's changing," said Evans more quietly. "I can feel it. Look," he pointed to the island, "the snow's thinning. That means the wind's picked up. Besides, feel the sea."

Martin noticed for the first time that the ship was tossing much more than it had an hour before. He had been daydreaming and had not noticed the gradual change.

Evans opened one of the windows and the familiar roar of wind and water filled the wheelhouse. Snowflakes flew in and melted quickly, leaving wet marks on the deck.

The snow flurries were disappearing and every moment the shores of the island became clearer. The sea was large though not yet dangerous.

"I don't like it," said Evans.

"Barometer's still low," said Martin helpfully.

"I know. Did we nest that boom, the one on the port side?"

"We did it last night, remember?"

"That's right. The hatches are pretty well battened down. . . ." Evans' voice trailed into silence.

A wave crashed over the bow and the whole ship shook. Martin slipped on the linoleum-covered deck; he caught himself before he fell. Evans was holding onto the wheel and did not lose his balance. The man at the wheel swung them back on course.

Through the open window blasts of wind whistled into the wheelhouse. Martin slammed the window shut. It was almost quiet with the window shut.

"You didn't want that open, did you?"

"No. Go write up our position and the barometer reading in the logbook."

Martin obeyed. When he had finished he stood by the telegraph.

"What do you think's happening?" he asked.

"I don't know. I haven't got any idea. Where's Bervick?"

"I think he went to the focs'le to get one of the men."

Evans swore loudly. "Why did you let him go up there? He should have stayed here. Why didn't he have sense to stay here?"

"What's the matter with you?" Martin was irritated. "What's so bad about his going there? It's none of my business."

"How," said Evans tightly, "do you think he's going to get back if the wind gets any worse? He's going to be stuck there and no damned use at all."

"That certainly's too bad," snarled Martin. "You want me to send out a carrier pigeon?"

Evans started to say something. He thought better of it, though. He walked across the slanting deck without speaking.

Martin, still angry, looked at the sea. He was surprised to see that the snow had almost stopped, and that black clouds hung in the sky and a strong wind was lashing the waves.

He turned around to speak to Evans and at that moment the williwaw hit the ship.

Martin was thrown across the wheelhouse. There was a thundering in his ears. He managed to grasp the railing and, desperately, he clung to it.

The wheelhouse hit the water with a creaking smack. For a minute the deck of the wheelhouse was at a right angle with the water. Then, slowly, the ship righted herself.

Evans, he saw, lay flat on the steep deck. The man who had been at the wheel was huddled near the companionway. The wheel was spinning aimlessly.

The ship shuddered as tremendous waves lifted her high in the air. Martin, confused and helpless, shut his eyes and wished that the huge sound of the wind would go away.

When he opened his eyes again he saw Evans crawling on hands and knees across the deck. Martin watched him move closer and closer to the wheel. A sudden lunge of the ship and Evans was thrown against it. Quickly he caught the wheel. Martin watched as Evans fought grimly to keep on course.

Through the windows, Martin could see what was happening. They were being driven toward the island. Evans was trying to hold them on any course away from shore.

Another jolt; a mountain of water swept over the wheelhouse. Evans was thrown against the bulkhead on the port side. Water streamed into the wheelhouse from new-made cracks.

Again the ship righted herself and again Evans started his slow crawl over the deck, only now the deck was slick with water. As the ship reached the crest of a wave Evans got to his feet and made a dash for the wheel. But this time he was flung against the door of the companionway. The man who had been at the wheel lay beside him.

Evans shouted something to Martin. The noise was too much and his voice did not carry. Evans gestured furiously with his hands. Martin understood him finally. Evans wanted the engines stopped.

Martin ran to the telegraph and, before a new wave hit them, he rang the engine room. Even in that moment he wondered what good it would do. He got back to his railing.

Luckily, Martin noticed, they were headed at an angle for the shore. They would not hit for a little while. He looked at Evans and saw that he was vomiting. He had never seen Evans sick before.

The wind, howling more loudly than ever, pushed them almost sideways at the island. The ship's side was held at a forty-five-degree angle. Once again, as Martin watched, Evans tried to get his hands on the wheel.

He got safely across the deck. Distantly, as though he were only an onlooker, Martin watched Evans struggle with the whirling wheel. Then there was a crash that shook the whole ship and Martin lost his grip on the railing.

He felt surprised, and that was all, as he was flung lightly to the other end of the wheelhouse. There was an explosion in his head and the last thing he saw was the dark blue-green of the bulkhead.

* * * *

Duval was sitting in the salon. Major Barkison, the Chaplain and Hodges were playing cards. Smitty was clearing away the lunch.

Duval was about to get up and go to his engine room when the whole ship seemed to turn upside down. He was pinned between the bench and the table.

Across the salon he saw the deck of cards scatter into the air. The Major, who had been sitting in a chair, was thrown heavily on the deck.

Hodges had fallen against one of the bulkheads. He was trying to find something to hold onto.

The Chaplain, like Duval, had been pinned between the bench and the table. His eyes were closed and his face very white. His lips were working quickly.

Slowly the ship righted herself. Duval thought of his engine room. He would have to get back to it. He started to move from behind the table but another gust of wind flattened the ship on the water. He relaxed and waited.

He was surprised at the force of the wind. It must be over a hundred ten miles an hour, he thought. He tried to think calmly. They would, of course, ride it out and then anchor somewhere.

Major Barkison staggered to his table and grasped it firmly. In the galley Duval could hear, even over the roar of the wind, the sound of crashing china. He noticed Smitty in the companionway, his feet braced against the bulkhead.

Hodges ran across the deck and sat down on the bench behind the Chaplain's table. The Chaplain's eyes were still closed, his face still pale.

The ship creaked and groaned and shuddered as the wind, almost capsizing her, pressed the port side to the sea.

Duval got to his feet. Holding the table tightly, he went toward the companionway. Then, when he was as close as he could get without letting go of the table, he jumped.

For a second he wondered if he had broken anything. He had tripped over Smitty and had fallen on the deck. He flexed his arms and legs. Nothing seemed to be wrong. Smitty, he could hear, was praying loudly.

Carefully the Chief worked his way down the companionway and into the engine room.

Each assistant was holding onto one of the engines. They were frightened. Duval pointed to the engines and raised his eyebrows in question: were they all right? The two men nodded.

He worked his way, without falling, back to his cabin. Everything that could have been broken was broken. Clothes were scattered over the deck. He sat on his bunk.

For the first time he noticed a pain in his knee. He felt the kneecap. Waves of pain shook him. He wondered if it was cracked and if so what he should do.

A sudden lurch of the ship and he forgot about his knee. He went back to the engine room. His assistants were still standing by.

The oiler who had been sick lay quietly on the deck. He had passed out.

Duval stood close to his first assistant. "No ring yet?" he yelled, pointing to the telegraph.

The man shook his head.

"Stop her O.K.?"

The man nodded.

There was a loud crash. Duval looked around and saw water trickling down the companionway. A porthole must have broken in the salon.

The Chief waited for Evans to ring instructions; he wondered if this was to be the way he would die. He had thought about it often, dying up in the islands. Everyone had thought about it. He had never thought, though, that he would come this close. New Orleans was a much better place to die.

The loud ring of the telegraph startled him. He nodded to his assistants. They spun the mechanism which stopped the engines. This done, the real wait began.

"Where we heading?" the man next to him shouted.

Duval thought a moment. He had not noticed and he did not know. He shook his head.

The same question was in each of their minds: were they heading for the island and the rocks? Those sharp tall rocks, much pounded by the sea.

He cursed himself for not having noticed. Just to know where they were going, without being able to do anything about it, was better than knowing nothing.

From above there came a loud splintering and a crash. He wondered what had happened. He wondered if he should go up on deck, but his knee was bothering him. He might not be able to get back.

The Chief held tightly to the engine as the ship rocked in the wind. He and his assistants waited. That was all they could do.

* * * *

Bervick had gone into the focs'le to get the fat cook.

Smitty had complained that he could not take care of lunch alone with the ship pitching.

Several men were in the focs'le. The fat cook was asleep in his bunk. Bervick shook him. "Come on and get up. You got to help out in the galley."

The fat cook yawned and swore. Slowly he hoisted himself out of the bunk. Bervick played with the dog.

"Hey, Bervick," said one of the men, "anything new going on? We're jumping around quite a bit. I thought the Skipper said there wasn't going to be no more storm."

"Looks like he's wrong. The sea's a lot bigger."

"You're telling me."

The fat cook was finally ready. They climbed the ladder to the main deck. Bervick looked out the port-hole. He could not believe what he saw. A high hill of gray-black water was sweeping down on them.

"Get down," he shouted to the cook who was below him on the ladder. They were too late. Both were thrown back into the focs'le.

The lights went out and in the darkness there were shouts from the surprised men. Bervick reached into his pocket and lit a match. Mattresses and blankets had been thrown against the port side. The men were clinging to the bunks. The match went out.

Guided by the pale gray light from the porthole above the ladder, Bervick climbed up again and looked out at the deck. The wind had blown the rigging loose from the mast and the ropes twisted in the air; many of them had been blown out to sea.

The ship was pressed close to the sea on the port side. The wheelhouse slapped the water with each new gust of wind. Waves, higher than he had ever seen before, swept over the decks. Water streamed over him from cracks in the deck.

Then Bervick saw that they were being driven toward the shore. The ship was out of control. No one could control her now.

Wind, almost visible in its strength, struck at the ship. One of the booms became loose. Horrified, Bervick watched it swing back and forth.

Quite easily the boom knocked the signal light off the top of the wheelhouse.

For a moment Bervick considered what his chances

were of reaching the wheelhouse in this wind. He dismissed the thought.

There was nothing he could do. If they hit the rocks there was little chance of any of them living. A person might last five minutes in the cold water. But the wind and waves would dash one to pieces faster than that.

He wondered what Evans was doing: probably trying to get control of the ship. When the wind was over a hundred miles an hour there was not much anyone could do but wait. That was what Evans would do. Stop the engines and wait.

The wind became more powerful every minute. The big wind was at its height. Great streams of wind-driven water battered the ship.

A large wave hit across their bow. Bervick stumbled and fell off the ladder. He rolled helplessly in the dark. There was a sudden snapping sound, louder than the wind. Then there was a crash. Bervick knew what had happened: the mast had been broken off. In the dark focs'le the dog began to whine.

* * * *

The mast was gone.

Evans had seen it splinter as the wind-rushed waves went over the ship.

The man on watch crouched near the wheel. He was trying to hold it, to stop it from spinning. Martin lay unconscious on the deck. As the ship rolled, his limp body skidded back and forth.

Only eight minutes had passed since the williwaw struck. To Evans it seemed as if the wind had been shouting in his ears for hours.

His mind was working quickly, though. He tried to figure what would be the best way to go aground if he got control of the ship. The best thing would be to hit at an angle.

He looked at the approaching shore. Ten minutes, perhaps a little longer: that was all the time he had and the wind was not stopping.

On the rocks the giant waves swirled and tumbled. A white mist rose from the shore, a mist of sea spray hiding the mountains behind the rocks. His stomach fluttered when he saw these rocks, black and sharp, formed in a volcanic time.

He wished Bervick was with him. He even wished that Martin was conscious. His mind raced to many things. He thought of a number of things. They came to him in quick succession, without reason.

Evans wondered if the fire was out in the galley range. If the electric generator was still working. What the ship's dog, whom he hated, was doing. Whether Duval still had his bandage on his finger and if not what the possibilities of blood poisoning were. He wondered what blood poisoning was like. His mother had died in childbirth; he thought of that.

The deckhand caught at the wheel and held it a moment. Then he had to let go. They could not even lash it secure. The ropes would break.

But the fact that the deckhand had managed to stop the wheel, even for a moment, gave Evans some hope.

Outside the sea was mountainous. Gray waves pushing steeply skyward, made valleys so deep that he could not see sky through the windows.

Evans hopped across the deck and grabbed the wheel. With all his strength he struggled to hold it still. The deckhand helped him hold the wheel. With both of them straining they managed to control the ship.

Ahead of them the shore of Kulak came closer. A long reef of rock curved out into the sea. Inside this curve the sea was quieter. They were running toward the end of the reef. They would strike it on their port bow.

Evans decided quickly to get inside the reef. It was the only thing to do.

"Hard to port," yelled Evans. The man helped push the wheel inch by inch to the left. Evans slipped but did not fall as a wave struck them. The deck was wet from the water which streamed in under the bulkheads.

Bits of rigging from the now vanished booms clattered on the wheelhouse windows. Luckily the windows had not been broken.

A gust of wind threw the ship into a wave. Both

Evans and the deckhand were torn loose from the wheel.

Evans was thrown into the chart table. He gasped. He could not breathe for several moments.

When he had got his breath back, Evans went to the window. Controlling the wheel was out of the question now. But they were inside the reef and that was good.

Evans held tightly to the railing. He watched the shore as they approached it.

Two tall rocks seemed to rush at him. Evans ducked quickly below the windows. They crashed into the rocks.

The noise was the worst thing. Breaking glass, as several windows broke. The almost human groan of the ship as the hull scraped on the rocks. The wind whistling into the wheelhouse and the thundering of water on the shore.

And then there was comparative quiet.

The wind still whistled and the sea was loud but the ship had stopped all motion.

Evans walked across the angled deck, and he was surprised at what he saw. The ship had been wedged between two rocks on the reef. The starboard side was somewhat lower than the port. The sea was deflected by one of the rocks and waves no longer rolled over the deck.

Martin, pale, his nose bleeding, walked unsteadily over to where Evans stood.

"We hit," he said.

"We hit," said Evans.

"How long I been out?"

"Maybe fifteen minutes."

"What're you going to do?"

"Wait till the storm stops."

Evans looked about him. The ship was securely wedged between the rocks. There did not seem to be much chance of being shaken loose. Evans shivered. He realized that he was very cold and that the wind was blowing through the two broken starboard windows.

He went into his cabin and put on his parka. His cabin, he noticed, was a tangled heap of clothes and papers and furniture.

He went back into the wheelhouse. "You stay here," he said to the deckhand. "Don't do anything. I'll be below for a while."

The galley was much the way he had expected it to be. Broken dishes on the deck and food and ashes littering the table and benches. Smitty sat silently amid the wreckage. He did not speak as Evans passed him.

The salon was in better shape: there had been fewer movable articles here. Still, chairs were scattered around in unlikely places and books were heaped on the deck.

Major Barkison sat limply on one of the benches. There were blue bruises on his face. He was flexing his hand carefully as though it hurt him.

Chaplain O'Mahoney sat very stiffly behind the table. His dark hair was in his eyes and sweat trickled down his face. He managed to smile as Evans entered.

Hodges, looking no worse for the storm, was peering out one of the portholes.

"Everyone all right?" Evans asked.

"I believe so," said the Chaplain. "We three aren't very damaged."

"Is it going to sink?" asked the Major, looking up.

"This ship? No, we're not going to sink. Not today anyway."

"What happened?" asked Hodges. "What did we hit?"

"We're stuck between two rocks inside a reef. We've been lucky."

"When are you going to get us out of here?" The Major was frightened. They were all frightened but the Major showed it more than the others.

"Just as soon as the wind lets up."

"Is that long?" asked Hodges.

"I don't know. There's a first aid kit in the galley locker." Evans went down the companionway and into the engine room.

Everything looked normal here. The two assistant engineers were checking their numerous gauges and the Chief was oiling a piece of machinery.

"What the hell did you hit?" asked the Chief. He did not seem bothered by what had happened and this annoyed Evans.

"We hit a rock, that's what we hit. How are the engines?"

"I think they're all right. The propellers aren't touching bottom and you can thank God that they aren't."

"Will she be able to go astern?"

"I don't see why not. Is that what we're going to do?"

"Yes."

"When do you want to push off?"

"When the wind stops."

"We'll have it ready."

Evans met Bervick in the salon. Bervick was wet from his dash across the open deck.

"What's the focs'le doing?" asked Evans. "Leaking?"

"No, we was lucky. We're hung up just under the bow. We've lost our guardrail and that's about all."

"Good." Evans looked through the after door. The sea crashed all around them, the white sea spray formed a cloud about them.

"Should be over soon," remarked Bervick. "I think it'll be over soon."

"Yes, it should be over," said Evans and he turned and walked back toward the wheelhouse.

iii

Bervick walked on the forward deck.

Since sundown the wind had almost died away. Water rippled about them and the ship creaked as she moved back and forth between the two rocks.

There was only a sharp stump where the mast had been. A few bits of rigging were scattered on the deck; for the most part the deck was clean of all debris.

One of the ventilators was gone and someone had covered up the hole where it had been with a piece of canvas. The other ventilator was slightly bent; otherwise, it was in good shape.

To his left rose the mountains of Kulak. They were like all the other mountains in the islands. The closer one was to them the more impressive they were.

He walked to the railing and leaned over and touched

the hard wet rock that shielded them from the last gusts of the wind.

Martin came slowly toward him. He walked unsurely. The knocking he had taken had weakened him.

"Here we are," he said.

Bervick nodded. "We got real messed up. It's the dry-dock for us if we get back."

"Hope we're sent to Seward. I like Seward."

"Nice town for Alaska. Maybe we'll get sent down to Seattle."

"My luck's not that good." Martin leaned over the railing and ran his hand over the shattered guardrail. "You think we'll get off these rocks all right?"

"I think so. Maybe we knocked a hole in the bottom. If that happened we got no chance."

"Maybe we didn't get a hole."

"That's the right idea."

They walked on the deck, looking for damage.

The cover to the anchor winch had blown away; the winch itself was not damaged.

"Let's go up top," said Martin. "Evans wants us to check the lifeboats."

The top of the wheelhouse was much battered. One of the two lifeboats was splintered and useless. Martin laughed.

"Those things aren't any use anyway, not up here they aren't."

"Sometimes you can get away."

"In a lifeboat like that?"

"Sure, it's been done."

"I wouldn't like to do that."

"Neither would I," Bervick tested the broken hull of the lifeboat with his hand. The wood creaked under the pressure.

"Let's go below," said Martin. "That's no good any more."

"I guess you're right."

They crossed the bridge and went into the wheelhouse. Evans was at the chart table. "What did you find?" he asked.

"One lifeboat knocked up and one ventilator on the forward deck gone," said Bervick.

"I saw the ventilator go," said Evans. "You say the lifeboat's out of commission?"

"That's right."

"Shipyard for us," said Evans and that was all. He turned back to his charts. Evans put on an act sometimes, thought Bervick.

"We're going below, Skipper," said Bervick and he and Martin left the wheelhouse.

Duval was in the salon. His coveralls were smeared with grease and he looked gaunt. He was sitting at the table, alone.

"When're we leaving this place?" he asked.

"Pretty soon," answered Bervick. "How're your engines?"

"I guess they'll be all right. You'll find out soon enough."

Bervick looked at the Chief's grease-stained coveralls. "You have some trouble?"

"One of the pumps stopped working. I think we got it fixed. The boys are testing it now."

"You look beat," commented Martin.

"You would be too. How did Evans manage to get us on the rocks, I wonder?"

"He didn't," said Bervick. "Just fool's luck that we got out of this thing this well."

"You mean so far," said the Chief sourly.

Bervick looked at him with dislike. Usually when they were working together there was no enmity but now, even on the rocks, he could not keep from disliking Duval.

"What's happened to the passengers?" asked Martin.

"Damned if I know. They've probably gone out on deck or hit their sacks. That Major certainly got excited."

"They all seemed excited," remarked Bervick.

"I suppose you weren't." The Chief stood up and sighed deeply. "I think I'll talk to Evans and see what's going to happen." He had started to leave when Evans came into the salon.

"When we going?" asked the Chief.

"Right away. Say, Martin, you take some men and go on deck and stand by while we go astern."

Martin left the salon. "Are you going to be able to handle the engines all right?" asked Evans, turning to the Chief.

"I think so. What're you going to do, go half speed astern?"

"Full speed, I think. Depends how tight we are. Come on, Bervick."

Someone had tacked pieces of canvas over the broken windows in the wheelhouse. "Handle the telegraph for me," said Evans.

"O.K." Bervick looked out the window and saw Martin with several deckhands. They were standing on the bow, waiting. Lieutenant Hodges was also on the forward deck.

Evans maneuvered the wheel for several moments. "Ring Stand By," he said at last. Bervick set the markers on Stand By. The Chief rang back quickly.

"Slow Astern," said Evans.

Bervick rang the engine room again. The regular throbbing of the engines began. The ship creaked and shifted slightly.

"Half Speed Astern," said Evans, his hands clutching the wheel tightly.

Bervick rang for Half Speed. The ship trembled. There was a ripping sound as they began to move from between the rocks. "There goes the guardrail," said Bervick.

"Full Speed Astern," said Evans.

Bervick set the markers on Full Speed. "Here we go," he said.

The ship, with much groaning as pieces of wood were torn from the bow, moved away from the rocks.

Evans swung the wheel hard to port. There was a suspended instant and then the bow splashed off the rocks. The ship rolled uncertainly for a moment. Then they were free.

"Cut the engines," said Evans.

The ship drifted away from shore.

"So far so good," said Evans. "Give her Slow Ahead." As the ship moved ahead Evans swung the bow out to sea.

"Now we can wait," he said.

"For the leaks to start?"

"For the leaks."

"Maybe I ought to go see the Chief, see how the pumps are working," suggested Bervick.

"Sure, go below."

The engine room was hot. Fumes from the engines made the air almost unbreathable. Duval was watching the gauges. His assistants stood beside the engines.

"Evans wants to know if the pumps are working."

"Tell him I think so. Got good pressure."

"I guess the engines weren't bothered at all."

"You can be glad of that."

Bervick went up to the salon. Martin was looking out the porthole at the island shore.

"We made it," said Bervick.

"Yes, we got off the rocks. I was afraid for a while we weren't going to be able to. We were really jammed in there. Took the whole guardrail off."

"Did you look in the focs'le to see if there were any leaks?"

"No. You think we should?"

"Yes. You take the focs'le and I'll go down in the hold."

On deck the wind was brisk but not strong. The air was clearer but the sky was still overcast. With night coming the weather might yet be good.

Bervick slipped the covering off one end of the hatch. Carefully he went down the narrow ladder. The hold was dark and damp and smelled of salt and wood. When he got to the bottom he turned on a light.

There were several crates of machinery on the deck of the hold. They had not been given much cargo to carry on this trip. Pieces of tarpaulin and lengths of line were strewn over the deck. Ammunition for the ship's gun rolled about the hold. They had dismantled most of their gun and had stored the pieces. No one ever saw the Japanese in these waters.

Bervick examined the damp bulkheads carefully. They seemed to be sound. He walked over the deck and could not find any sign of a leak.

He turned off the light and climbed out of the hold. Martin was standing by the railing.

"Find anything?" Bervick asked.

Martin shook his head. "Everything fine. You find anything?"

"No." They went aft to the salon. Martin went above to tell Evans about their inspection.

Major Barkison was in the salon when Bervick entered. He was nervous; his fingers played constantly with his belt buckle.

"Do you think it's over for good?" he asked.

"I expect so. The heart of the storm's gone by us."

"I hope so. That was really dreadful, the rocks and all that wind. Does this happen often?"

"Occasionally it happens."

"It was awful. We'll get back all right now, though. Won't we?"

"I hope so. Evans is good, he knows his business. I wouldn't be too worried."

"No, I suppose it's all over." The Major shuddered. "That wind, I've never seen anything like it. It was terrible, all that wind." The Major sat down heavily.

Evans came into the salon. He seemed cheerful. He was smiling.

"Martin tells me there aren't any leaks."

Bervick nodded, "That's right."

"We'll get there then. I'm hungry. Is Smitty around?"

"I think he's below. I'll get him."

"Fine."

"I gather," said the Major slowly, "that the storm is over."

"Well, it looks like it. Never can tell, of course. We may have some more but the worst is over."

Major Barkison was relieved. "You know," he said, "I must admire the way you've handled this. I'm going to recommend you for a citation."

Evans laughed, "Send me back to the States, that's what I want."

"I'm serious," said the Major. "You've done a remarkable job and we are all, naturally, most grateful."

There was an embarrassed silence. Bervick looked at Evans and saw that Evans was at a loss to say anything. Evans did not know how to say the right things.

"I'll get Smitty up," said Bervick.

"Fine," said Evans. "Go get him up. I'm hungry."

Bervick found Smitty in his bunk. "Come on and get up," he said. "We want some chow."

Smitty swore loudly. "I seen everything now," he said and he got out of his bunk.

Bervick went back to the salon.

Chapter Six

i

THEY had steak for supper. Smitty, in a mood of thanksgiving, had cooked an unusually good meal. He served it himself, almost cheerfully.

"Such a nice quiet evening," exclaimed the Chaplain.

"It's a real relief," said the Major. "A real relief. I thought for a while that . . . well, that that was it, if you know what I mean."

"It was pretty close," said Evans, smiling. His passengers looked much better. The Chaplain especially seemed happy.

"Yes," said the Major, "I think we've been lucky. Of course, we have Mr Evans here to thank. If it hadn't been for his . . . his efforts, I suppose, we'd be dead now."

"That's right," said the Chaplain, looking fondly at Evans. "You really did a remarkable job."

"Pass the sugar," said Duval and he took the sugar when it was passed to him and put several spoonsful of it in his coffee. Evans could see that he did not like to hear his Skipper praised.

"By the way," said Evans, "I think we should really compliment the Chief. He sure did a good job. If his engine room hadn't been operating I don't know where we'd be."

"That's right," said the Major, "we mustn't forget Mr Duval."

"We've been extremely fortunate," said the Chaplain. "Not of course that we all weren't quite ready to . . . to meet our Maker, as it were."

122

"I wasn't," said Hodges abruptly. The others laughed.

"Tell me, Mr Evans," said the Major, "when do you expect to get to Arunga?"

"Tomorrow sometime, afternoon, I guess. Depends on what kind of time we make."

"Excellent."

"By the way," said the Chief, "that ventilator, the one over the starboard engine; water and everything else's been coming down it. You get someone to fix it?"

Evans nodded; he looked at Bervick. "You want to take care of that?"

"Sure."

Evans sat down on one of the long benches that lined the bulkheads. Martin was in the wheelhouse. They were on course and the barometer was rising.

He shut his eyes and relaxed. The rocking of the ship was gentle and persistent. He had had an operation once and he had been given ether. There were terrible dreams. . . . All through the dreams there had been a ticking, a heartbeat rhythm, and a floating sensation much like the sea. He began to recall the dream. He was happy, and when he was happy he enjoyed torturing himself in a subtle fashion. He pretended that he was under the ether again, that the rocking of the ship was the dream. He recalled objects that looked like straws set in a dark green background. Lights shone from the tops of the straws and deep deep voices speaking in a Negro manner came out of the tips of the straws. He began to sink into the vastness of the ether dream. There was a struggle and then a sense of being alone, of being overcome. The deep voices kept throbbing in his ears. Then there was quiet.

*　　*　　*　　*

"Did you have a nice nap?" asked the Chaplain.

Evans opened his eyes and tried to look alert. "Just dozing." He sat up. The Chaplain and he were the only ones in the salon. He looked at his watch: it was after ten.

"I cannot," said the Chaplain, "get over the great change in the weather."

"In the williwaw season weather does funny things."

"I had what you might call a revelation of sorts, if you know what I mean, during the storm."

"Is that right?" Evans wondered who was on watch. It was supposed to be his watch until midnight. Bervick had probably taken over while he slept.

"I had a sort of vision, well not quite a vision, no, not a vision, a presentiment, yes, that's what I had, a presentiment of something."

"Did you?" Evans was not sure that he knew what a presentiment was.

"This vision, presentiment I should say, was about the ship."

"Well, what was it?"

"Nothing much at all. It's really quite vague to me now. It was only that we'd all get out of this, that no one would be hurt on the trip, that's all. That's why I suppose one would call it a presentiment. It was just a feeling of course. A kind of instinct."

"Is that right? I've had them too." Evans wondered if the ventilator was still leaking.

"Have you really? I know there's a sort of intuition, a sort of sixth sense I would suppose you'd call it."

"Sure, that's what I'd call it." Evans wondered if there was anything to religion. Probably not, at least he himself had gotten along without it. He tried to recall if he'd ever been inside a church. He could not remember. In the back of his mind there was a feeling of great space and peacefulness which might have been the memory of a childhood visit to a church. He had seen some movies, though, that had church interiors in them. Churches where gray-haired men in long black robes stood in what appeared to be upright coffins and talked interminably about large resonant things. He had learned about religion from the movies and from the Chaplains he had met.

The Chaplain, his sixth sense at work, guessed what he was thinking. "You are not particularly, ah, religious, are you, Mr Evans."

"Well, I wouldn't say that," said Evans, who would have said just that if he had not disliked being thought different from other people.

"Oh no, I can tell that you're a . . . a pagan." The Chaplain chuckled to show that this epithet was not serious.

"I hope not." Evans was not too sure what "pagan" meant, either. He wished that people would use simple familiar words. That was the main thing he disliked in Martin: the long words that sounded as if they meant something very important.

"Well, there are many, many people like you in the world," said Chaplain O'Mahoney sadly, aware suddenly of the immensity of sin, the smallness of virtue.

"I guess there are." Evans wondered if Martin had recorded the rising barometer readings regularly.

"Did you ever feel lost?" asked the Chaplain in an almost conspiratorial tone.

"What? Well, I don't know."

"I mean did you ever feel lonely?"

"Certainly, haven't you?"

The Chaplain was a little startled, then he answered quickly, "No, never. You see I have something to fall back on."

"I suppose you do," said Evans and he tried to sound thoughtful and sincere but he managed only to sound bored.

The Chaplain laughed. "I'm being unfair, talking to you like this when your mind's on the ship and . . . and things."

"No, no, that's all right. I'm very interested. I once wanted to be a preacher." Evans added this for the sake of conversation.

"Indeed, and why didn't you become one?"

Evans thought a moment. Pictures of gray-haired men in black robes and gray-haired men advertising whiskey in the magazines were jumbled together in his inner eye. He had never become a minister for the simple reason that he had never been interested. But the thought that was suddenly the most shocking to him was that he had never wanted to *become* anything at all. He had just wanted to do what he liked. This was a revelation to him. He had thought about himself all his life but he had never been aware that he was different from most people. He just wanted to sail because he liked to sail and he wanted to get married again because it seemed like a comfortable way to live. Chaplains and Majors wanted to become Saints and Generals respectively.

"I guess I never really wanted to be a minister very much." Evans ran his hand through his hair. He noticed it was getting long. He would have a haircut when they got to Arunga.

"Some, I suppose," said the Chaplain philosophically, "are chosen, while others are not."

"Isn't that the truth?" said Evans with more emphasis than was necessary.

The Chaplain squinted his eyes and took a deep breath and Evans could see that he was going to be lectured. He stood up and the Chaplain, looking surprised, opened his eyes again and exhaled, a slight look of disappointment on his face.

"If you'll excuse me I'm going up top. My watch's now."

"Of course, certainly."

Bervick was standing by the windows, looking out. Evans stood beside him and they watched the sea together. The dark water shifted lazily now, gusts of wind occasionally ruffling the surface of the water. The night sky was black.

"You been asleep?"

Evans nodded.

"That's what I thought. Martin hit the sack."

"Barometer's up."

"That's nice. I don't like low barometers."

"Nobody likes them."

Evans looked at the stump where the mast had been. "She really tore off hard, didn't she?"

"Glad I wasn't under it."

"I guess the boys'll really talk about us now, the guys on the other boats."

"Sure, they're just like women. Talk, talk, that's about all they do."

"I guess they'll say it was my fault. Harms would say that. He'd want to cover his own hide for sending us out."

"Well, you didn't have to go if you didn't want to. That's sea law."

"That's true."

"But I don't think they're going to say it was your fault. Worse things've happened to a lot of other guys."

"It wasn't my fault, this thing, was it?"

"I don't think so. You ain't no weather prophet."

"There wasn't any way for me to tell that there'd be a williwaw."

"Well, this is the season for them."

"But how could I know that it was going to happen? We were cleared at the Big Harbor."

"It's on their neck then."

"I hope so, it'd better be. I couldn't help it if we got caught like that, got caught in a williwaw."

"Sure, sure, it was no fault of yours."

Evans looked out of the window. He was getting a little worried. The thought that he might be held responsible for taking a boat out and getting it wrecked in williwaw weather was beginning to bother him. Bervick was soothing, though.

"You taking over now?" he said.

Evans nodded, "Yes, I'll take over. You got a couple of hours, why don't you get some sleep?"

"I think I'll go below and mess around. I'm not so sleepy."

"By the way, did you fix that ventilator, the one over the Chief's engine room?"

Bervick frowned, "No, I forgot all about it. I'll go now." Bervick left the wheelhouse. Evans checked the compass with the course. Then he opened one of the windows and let the cool air into the wheelhouse. In a few minutes he would go to his cabin and take a swallow of bourbon; then he would come back and feel much happier as he stood his watch and thought.

ii

Major Barkison and the Chaplain were in the salon when Bervick entered. The Chaplain was putting on his parka.

"Hello, Sergeant," said the Major. "We thought we might take a stroll on deck before turning in."

"It's pretty windy still."

"Well," said the Chaplain, "I wouldn't want to get a chill on top of all this excitement."

"Well," said the Major, "maybe we'd better just go to our cabins." The Chaplain thought that was a good idea and Bervick was glad to see them go.

He walked around the salon, straightening chairs and arranging the books which were still scattered about. The salon was quiet, now that the big wind had stopped. Even the bare electric lights seemed more friendly than usual.

The after door opened and Hodges came into the salon. He slammed the door and stood shivering as the heat of the salon warmed him.

"What were you doing out?" asked Bervick.

"Walking around. I think we'll be able to see stars soon. Looks like it's clearing up."

"Going to be quite a while before she clears that much."

"Well, it looked pretty clear to me."

"Clouds thinning maybe. I'll be on deck myself soon."

"You'll see nice weather, at least that's what I saw." Hodges sat on the bench and scratched his leg thoughtfully.

"Hope so." Bervick tried to think why he had come below. He looked up and saw that Duval was standing near him; he remembered.

The Chief was angry, "Say, Bervick, I thought you was going to fix that ventilator."

"What's the matter with it now, we ain't rocking much."

"Well, it's leaking all over my engine, that's what's the matter. I thought Evans told you to get that fixed long time ago?"

"He certainly did. You heard him, too, I guess," Bervick tried to irritate Duval.

"Damn it then, what're you going to do, just stand there like a stupid bastard?"

Bervick frowned. "You watch what you say, Chief."

"Who do you think you are telling me what I should say, anyhow?"

"Let's take it easy," said Hodges, remembering his superior rank and deciding that things were getting out of hand.

Bervick and the Chief ignored him. "I don't want you calling me a bastard," said Bervick. He enjoyed himself, fighting with Duval like this. Somehow Duval had begun to represent everything that he hated.

"I'll call you anything I like when you sound off like that. You think you're pretty smart, don't you? Hanging around Evans all the time. You and he think you're mighty superior to everybody else."

"We sure in hell are to you."

Duval flushed a dirty red. "Shut up, you thick square-head."

"Cajun!" Bervick snarled the word, made an oath of it.

Duval started toward him. Hodges stood up. "By the way," said Hodges quickly, "where are the Major and the Chaplain?"

"What?" Duval stopped uncertainly; then he remembered himself. "I don't know."

"They've gone to bed," said Bervick. He was sorry that the Chief had not tried to fight with him.

Hodges, pleased that he had stopped what could have been serious trouble, tried to think of something else to say. He asked, "Do you get into the Big Harbor often, Mr Duval?" This was the first thing that came into his head and it was the wrong thing to say.

"Yeah, we go there once, twice a week," said Duval.

"A lot of nice people there," said Bervick, looking at Duval.

"All you got to have is money," said the Chief softly, "money and technique, that's all you've got to have. Some people ain't got either."

"You're right there," said Bervick. "Some people got just one and not the other. Some people that I could name are just like that."

"Some people," said Duval, beginning to enjoy himself, "haven't got nothing to offer. I pity those people, don't you, Lieutenant?"

Hodges, somewhat puzzled, agreed that he pitied those people.

"Of course," said Bervick, "there are some guys who sneak around and get other people's girls and give them a lot of money when they get too old to give anything else."

This stung Duval but he did not show it. "Sure, sure, then there're the big snow artists. They talk all the time, that's all they do is talk. That's what Olga said someone we know used to do all the time, talk."

"You must've made that up. Maybe she meant you. Yes, that's who she meant, she meant you."

"I don't think so. She knows better. This guy was a squarehead, the guy she was talking about."

"I think," said Hodges, worried by the familiar pattern of the argument, "I think maybe you better take care of that ventilator, like you said."

"That's right," said Bervick, "we can't let the spray get on the Chief Engineer. That's getting him too near the water."

"I been on boats before you was born."

"Sure, they have ferries where I come from, too."

There was silence. Bervick felt keen and alive and strangely excited, as though something important was going to happen to him. He looked at the Chief in an almost detached manner. Hodges was frowning, he noticed. Hodges was very young and not yet able to grasp the problems of loneliness and rivalry.

"Someday," said the Chief at last, "somebody's going to teach you a lesson."

"I can wait."

"I think it would be a good idea," said Hodges, "if you went and fixed whatever you have to fix. You're not getting anywhere now."

"O.K.," said Bervick, "I'll fix it."

"You going to do it alone?" asked Hodges.

"Sure, it's too late to get anybody else to help. I couldn't ask the Chief because he's too high-ranking to do any work."

"Shut up," said the Chief. "I could do it alone if I wanted to."

"Then why don't you?"

"Why," said Hodges, "don't you do it together?" At Officers' School they had taught him that nothing brought men closer together than the same work.

"That's a fine idea," said Bervick, knowing that Duval would not like it.

"Sure," said the Chief, "sure."

They walked out on deck. Hodges stayed in the salon, playing solitaire.

There was a cold wind blowing and the ship was pitching on the short small waves. Spray splattered the decks from time to time. The sky was beginning to clear a little. Hodges had been right about the weather.

The ventilator was dented and slightly out of position. When spray came over the side of the ship it eddied around the base of the ventilator and water trickled through to the engine room.

Duval and Bervick looked at the ventilator and did not speak. Bervick pushed it and felt it give slightly. Duval sat on the railing of the ship, opposite the ventilator.

"I suppose," said Bervick, "we should hammer the thing in place."

"You go get the hammer then."

Bervick walked to the afterdeck. He leaned down and raised the lid of the lazaret. A smell of tar and rope came to him from the dark hole. He climbed down inside the lazaret and fumbled around a moment in the dark. Then he found a hammer and some nails.

"What took you so long?" asked the Chief. He was standing by the ventilator, smoking.

"You forgot about blackout rules, huh? You making your own smoking rules now?"

"You just mind your business." Duval went on smoking calmly.

"I'm going to tell Evans," said Bervick.

"You do just what you please. Now let's fix that ventilator and stop talking."

Bervick got down on his knees and tried to wiggle the ventilator in place. It was too heavy. He stood up again.

"What's the matter? Can't you get it in place?"

"No, I'd like to see you try."

The Chief got down on his knees and pushed at the ventilator. Nothing happened. In the darkness Bervick could see the lighted tip of the Chief's cigarette blinking quickly as he puffed. Duval stood up.

"You have to move these things from the top, that's what you have to do."

"Well, why don't you?"

"That's what you're on this boat for, to take care of them things like that. You're a deckhand and this is deck work. This isn't my job."

"You're the one that's complaining. It don't make no difference to me if your engine gets wet."

Duval tossed his cigarette overboard. "Take care of that." He pointed to the ventilator.

Bervick slowly pushed the ventilator over the opening it was to cover. Then he picked up the hammer and started to nail the base of the ventilator into the deck.

"How's it coming?" asked a voice. Bervick looked up and recognized Hodges. He was standing beside the Chief.

"Don't know yet. Trying to nail this thing down." He was conscious that his knees were aching from the cold damp deck. He stood up.

"What's the matter now?" asked Duval.

"Knees ache."

"You got rheumatism, maybe?" asked Hodges with interest.

"Everybody has a little bit of it up here," said Bervick and he rubbed his knees and wished the pain would go away.

"I never had it," said the Chief as though it were something to be proud of.

"Why, I thought I saw you limping around today," said Hodges.

"That was a bang I got in the williwaw. Just bruised my knee."

"Well, I'll see you all later." Hodges walked toward the forward deck. The ship was pitching more than usual. The waves were becoming larger but overhead the sky was clearing and there was no storm in sight.

"Let's get this done," said Duval, "I'm getting cold."

"That's too bad. Maybe if you did some work you'd warm up."

"Come on," said Duval and he began to wrestle with the ventilator. It was six feet tall, as tall as Duval.

"That's no way to move it," said Bervick. He pushed the Chief away and he grasped the ventilator by the top. Slowly he worked it into place again. Duval watched him.

"See how simple it is," said Bervick.

Duval grunted and sat down on the railing again. Overhead a few stars began to shine very palely on the sea. Bervick hammered in the dark. Then, working too quickly, he hit his own hand. "Christ!" he said and dropped the hammer.

"Now what's wrong?" asked Duval irritably, shifting his position on the railing.

"Hit my hand," said Bervick, grasping it tightly with his good hand.

"Well, hurry up and get that thing nailed."

Anger flowed through Bervick in a hot stream. "Damn it, if you're in a hurry, do it yourself." He picked up the hammer and threw it at Duval.

The hammer, aimed at Duval's stomach, curved upward and hit him in the neck. The Chief made a grab for the hammer and then the ship descended into a trough.

Duval swayed uncertainly on the railing. Then Duval fell overboard.

There was a shout and that was all. Bervick got to his feet and ran to the railing. He could see the Chief, struggling in the cold water. He was already over a hundred feet away. Bervick watched him, fascinated. He could not move.

His mind worked rapidly. He must find Evans and stop the engines. Then they would get a lifeboat and row out and pick the Chief up. Of course, after five, ten minutes in the water he would be dead.

Bervick did not move, though. He watched the dark object on the water as it slipped slowly away. The ship sank into another deep trough and when they reached the crest of the next wave there was no dark object on the water.

Then he was able to move again. He walked, without thinking, to the forward deck. A wet wind chilled his face as he looked out to sea. The snow clouds were still thinning. In places dim stars shone in the sky.

He walked back to the stump where the mast had been. He felt the jagged wood splinters and was glad that he had not been under the mast when it had fallen.

Slowly Bervick walked to the afterdeck. He had left the lazaret open; he closed it and then he went into the salon.

Hodges was building a house of cards. His hands were very steady and he was working intensely. When Bervick shut the door the house of cards collapsed.

"Damn," said Hodges and smiled. "Get it fixed all right?" he asked.

"Yeah, we got it fixed."

"I thought I heard a splash a minute ago. You drop anything over?"

Bervick swallowed hard. "No, I didn't throw nothing overboard."

"I guess it was just waves hitting the boat."

"Yeah, that was it, waves hitting the deck." Bervick sat down on a bench and thought of nothing.

"Where'd the Chief go?" asked Hodges.

Bervick wished that Hodges would shut up. "I think he went below. He went around outside." Once the lie was made things became clearer to Bervick. They wouldn't know what had happened for hours.

Hodges began to build his house of cards again.

Light glinted for a moment on Hodges' gold ring. That reminded Bervick of something. He was puzzled. It reminded him of something unpleasant and important. Then he remembered: the Chief's gold tooth which always gleamed when he laughed, when he laughed at Bervick. Duval was dead now. He realized this for the first time.

The salon was very still. Bervick could hear the careful breathing of Hodges as he built his house of cards. Bervick watched his fingers, steady fingers, as he worked.

No one would be sorry Duval was dead, thought

Bervick. His wife would be, of course, and his family, but the men wouldn't. They'd think it was a fine thing. They would talk about it, of course. They would try to guess what had happened, how Duval fell overboard; they would wonder when it had happened.

"You and the Chief were really arguing," commented Hodges, putting a piece of the roof in place.

"We're not serious."

"You sounded serious to me. It's none of my business but I think maybe you sounded off a little too loud. He's one of your officers."

"We didn't mean nothing. He talked out of line, too."

"That's right. That's dangerous stuff to do, talk out of line. There can be a lot of trouble."

"Sure, a lot of trouble. Sometimes guys kill each other up here. It's happened. This is a funny place. You get a little queer up here."

"I suppose you're right." Hodges added a third story to his house.

"Me and the Chief, we don't get along so well, but I ain't got any hard feelings against him, know what I mean?"

"I think so. Started over a girl, didn't it?"

"There're not many up here. The ones they've got there's a lot of competition for. We were just after the same one."

"He got her?"

"Yeah, he got her."

Hodges began to build an annex on the left side of the house. Bervick hoped he would build one on the right side, too. It looked lopsided the way it was.

"That's too bad," said Hodges.

"I didn't like it so much, either."

"I know how you feel."

Bervick doubted that, but said nothing.

Hodges decided to build a fourth story. The house of cards collapsed promptly. "Damn," said Hodges and he did not rebuild.

Bervick looked at his watch. "I'd better get some sleep," he said. "See you in the morning."

"Yeah, see you."

Evans was singing to himself when Bervick came into the wheelhouse. The man at the wheel looked sleepily out to sea.

"Fix the ventilator?"

"Yes."

"Have much trouble with it?"

"Not so much."

"Hammer it?"

"We hammered it."

"Who helped you? Not the Chief?"

"Well, he stood by and watched."

"Was he sore you hadn't already done it?"

"He's always sore about something."

"I thought I heard you and him arguing below."

Bervick played with his blond hair. "We had a little argument about fixing the ventilator."

"I'll bet you sounded off right in front of the Major."

"No, just Hodges."

Evans groaned, "What the hell's matter with you? Can't you get along any better than that with people?"

"Doesn't look much like it."

"He's going to try to get you off this boat, you know that?"

"I don't think he will," said Bervick and he was sorry he had spoken so quickly.

"What do you mean?"

"Oh, you know, I don't think he's that kind of guy."

"I never heard you say that before."

"Well, he's not so bad, when you get to know him."

"Is that right?" Evans laughed. "You don't make much sense."

Bervick laughed. It was the first time that he had really felt like laughing in several months. The surface of his mind was serene; only in the back of his mind, the thoughts he was not thinking about, only there was he uneasy.

"Martin taking over at eight bells?"

Evans nodded. "You better get him up."

Bervick went into the small dark cabin. Martin was asleep and breathing heavily. Bervick shook him.

"Get up," he said.

"Sure, sure," said Martin wearily. He rolled out of his bunk; he was already dressed.

"Afraid we might sink?"

"Sure, sure," said Martin and he moved unsteadily to the wheelhouse.

Bervick sat down on his bunk and looked at the darkness. Duval was dead. He imagined how it must have felt: the cold water, the numbing sensation, desperation, and then the whole elaborate business of living ended.

Evans opened the door of his cabin. "You asleep?" he asked.

"No."

"I'm going below now. Which ventilator did you fix? I've forgot."

"The starboard side. The one amidship."

"That's what I thought."

"You going below now?"

"I thought I'd look around before I turned in. Chief still up?"

Bervick controlled his breathing very carefully. "No. He said he was going to hit the sack."

"I won't bother him then. Good night."

"Night." Evans closed the door.

Bervick lay in the darkness. He rolled from side to side in his bunk as the ship lunged regularly on the waves.

It was not his fault. He was sure of that. He had handed Duval the hammer. Well, he had thrown the hammer to him. He had not thrown it very hard, though. The Chief had lost his balance, that was all. Perhaps the hammer had hit him and thrown him off balance, but that was not likely. The ship had been hit by a wave and he was on the railing and fell off. Of course, the hammer might have been thrown much harder than he thought, but Duval had caught it all right. Well, perhaps he had not quite caught it; the hammer had hit him in the neck, but not hard enough to knock him overboard.

Then Duval was in the water and Bervick had tried to get help but it was too late. No, that was not right, he had not tried to get help: he had only stood there.

But what could he have done? Fifteen minutes would have passed before they could have rescued him. Duval would have been frozen by then. Of course, he should have tried to pick him up. They couldn't lose time, though. Not in this weather. He had tried throwing Duval a line; no, that wasn't true at all. He had done nothing at all.

They would find he was gone by morning, or sooner. Then they would talk. Hodges would try to remember when Duval had left and he would remember hearing a splash: the hammer falling overboard. The Chief had gone back to the engine room or some place like that.

Bervick slept uneasily. From time to time he would awaken with a start, but he could not remember his dreams. That was the trouble with dreams. The sensation could be recalled but the details were lost. There were so many dreams.

iii

"I don't see how it happened," said the Major. "It's been so calm."

"I know, it's been very calm," agreed the Chaplain.

Major Barkison, the Chaplain and Hodges were in the salon. A half-hour before, at three-thirty in the morning, Evans had told them that Duval was missing.

In the galley the crew was gathered. The passengers could hear their voices as Evans questioned them.

Hodges sat at the galley table playing solitaire. He had been asleep when one of the crew had come and asked him to see Evans in the salon.

Hodges was sleepy. He hoped that Evans would finish his questioning soon and let them go back to bed. It was exciting, of course, to have a man disappear, and he wondered what had happened. Hodges could not believe that Duval had fallen overboard. That was too unlikely. That couldn't happen to anyone he had talked to such a short time before.

"The decks are quite slick," commented the Major. "It's easy to slip on them; all you have to do is slip and that's the end."

"I can't believe it happened that way," said the Chaplain. "He must be somewhere around the ship. There must be a lot of places where he could be." The Chaplain, like Hodges, could not grasp sudden death.

"This isn't a big ship," said the Major serenely. "They must've looked everywhere."

"That water must be awfully cold," said Hodges, beginning to feel awake.

The Chaplain shuddered and muttered something under his breath.

"Almost instant death," said the Major. "Almost instant death," he repeated softly. The Chaplain crossed himself. Hodges wondered how the water must have felt: the killing waves.

Evans and Martin walked in from the galley. Evans looked worried.

"Did any of you people see Duval tonight?" he asked.

The Major and the Chaplain said they had not.

"I did," said Hodges.

"About when?"

"Around ten or eleven, I guess, I haven't kept much track of time lately."

"What was he doing?"

"Well, he and Bervick were arguing about fixing the ventilator or something."

"I know all about that. Did you see him around later?"

"No. He and Bervick went outside to fix this thing. Bervick came back in alone. He said something or other about the Chief going below."

Evans sat down on the bench. The lines in his face were deep now. He seemed to Hodges to have stood about all he could. First the williwaw and then this.

"Go get Bervick," said Evans, turning to Martin. Martin left.

"I guess he fell off, if he did fall off, after Bervick came in," said Hodges.

"Could be," said Evans.

"I can't really believe this has happened," said the Chaplain. "He must be somewhere on the ship."

"I wish he were," said Evans. "I wish he were."

"There will probably be an investigation," said the Major.

Evans nodded. "They'll be running all over the ship."

Bervick and Martin joined them. Bervick looked surprised.

"Chief's missing. That right?"

"Yeah, he's gone. The Lieutenant here didn't see the Chief after you and him went out to fix the vent."

Bervick nodded. "We went out and when we finished the Chief said something about going up forward. I went on back to the salon. I guess he went on below later."

"Or else he fell overboard after you left," commented Evans. He turned again to Martin, "Get the assistants, will you?"

The assistant engineers were as surprised as the rest.

"I don't know nothing about it," said the heavy-set one. "Chief, he went on up top around ten o'clock and he didn't come back down, or at least I didn't see him again." The other assistant had not seen him either.

"Well, there's the story," said Evans. "On his way back he must have slipped."

"But it wasn't rough at all," said the Major. "I wonder how he managed to fall over." The Major carefully made his large-nosed profile appear keen and hawklike.

"Well, he'd been sitting on the railing when I was fixing the ventilator. He might have sat on the forward railing after I left," said Bervick.

"He could lose his balance then?"

Bervick nodded, "Easiest thing in the world."

"I see."

"We had a deckhand fall off that way once."

"Of course, that's what I feel must have happened. The decks are so slick."

"And you can lose your balance on a railing."

"I suppose so."

The Chaplain was calm now. He remembered his duty as a priest. "There will have to be some sort of service," he said, looking at Evans.

"That's right," Evans agreed. "I'm supposed to give

it but if you wouldn't mind I'd rather have you take care of it."

"That's perfectly all right. I should be glad to give the service."

"What kind is it?" asked the Major dubiously.

"The Burial at Sea one," said Evans. "Masters of ships are supposed to read it when one of the men dies at sea."

"Do you have a copy somewhere?" asked the Chaplain. "I'm afraid I don't know it. Not quite in my line, you know."

"Yeah, I've a copy up top." Evans looked into the galley. "Hey, Jim," he said, "go up and get that Manual, the gray one on my desk."

There was loud grumbling from Jim as he obeyed.

"Will you make a sermon?" asked the Major.

"No, I don't think so. Well, perhaps."

Hodges could see that the Chaplain was rising to the occasion with considerable gusto.

"Perhaps a short prayer after the service. Something very simple, something to describe our, ah, thankfulness and so on."

"That will be nice," said Major Barkison.

"Yes, after all it's our duty to do this thing right."

"I'll bet the Chief would get a kick out of this," commented Martin.

Bervick, who was standing beside him, nodded. "Chief would really like all this attention."

Hodges sat beside Evans on the bench. "What kind of report you going to make, Mr Evans?"

Evans shrugged. "The usual one, I guess. Lost at sea in line of duty, accident."

"That's the simplest, I suppose." Hodges looked at the others. They were very solemn. Death had a sobering effect on people: reminded them that they were not immortal.

The Chaplain sat muttering to himself. Hodges wondered if the Chaplain enjoyed this sudden call on his professional services.

Major Barkison, whom Hodges admired, was indifferent, or at least he seemed indifferent. His face was cold and severe. Hodges tried to look cold and severe, too.

Martin was excited. His face was flushed and his eyes unusually bright. He talked with Bervick who seldom answered him.

Hodges tried to remember something. He was reminded of this thing by the sound of waves splashing on the deck. He scowled and thought and concentrated but the thing floated away from his conscious mind.

Evans was talking to one of the assistant engineers. "I want you to get the Chief's stuff together. I'll have to inspect it and then we'll send it back."

"I'll get the stuff together." The two engineers were less moved than any of the others.

Evans turned to Martin, "You better make out that usual notice, you know the one about all people owed money by the Chief, that one."

"I'll write it up tomorrow."

The deckhand named Jim returned and gave Evans a flat gray book.

"Here's the book," said Evans.

"Oh, yes." The Chaplain stood up and Evans handed him the book. The Chaplain thumbed through the pages muttering, "Fine, fine," to himself. "A very nice Burial," he announced at last. "One of the best. I suggest you call the men together."

Evans nodded at Bervick and Bervick went into the galley. The Chaplain took his place at the head of one of the tables. Evans stood beside him. Hodges joined Martin and the Major at the far end of the salon.

The crew wandered in. There was a low growl of voices as they talked among themselves. Bervick assembled them in front of the Chaplain. Then he stood beside Evans.

"Everybody's here except the man on watch."

"O.K.," said Evans. "You want to start, Chaplain?"

The Chaplain nodded gravely. "I wish," he said in a low voice, "that I had my, ah, raiment."

"It's in the hold," said Evans. "I don't think we could get it."

"Perfectly all right."

Hodges strained to remember the thing that hovered

in the back of his mind; the thought that made him uneasy.

The Chaplain was speaking. He was saying how sad it was that Duval was dead.

Hodges watched the Chaplain. He seemed to expand, to become larger. His voice was deeper and the words came in ordered cadences.

He began to speak:

"Unto Thy Mercy, most Merciful Father, we commend the soul of our brother departed, and we commit his body to the deep; in sure and certain hope of the resurrection to eternal life through our Lord Jesus Christ.

"I heard a voice from Heaven saying. . . ."

Hodges looked at Bervick. His face was tired. A wave hit over the ship; there was a splashing sound.

The Chaplain began to speak Latin and Hodges looked at Bervick again.

Chapter Seven

i

"Snow's starting to clear," said Martin.

Evans looked up from the chart table. "We'll see Arunga when the snow clears."

A high wind had sprung up during the afternoon and snow flurries swept by them constantly. For a while Martin had been afraid there would be another williwaw, but now that they were so near to Arunga it made no difference. A williwaw near port was much different from one at sea.

Martin watched Evans as he measured distances on the chart with a pair of dividers. Already he was relaxed. He was whistling to himself.

"Looks like we're going to make it," said Martin.

"I guess so." Evans did not look up from his chart.

"That williwaw, that was pretty close, wasn't it? I mean we were almost knocked out."

"I'll say." Evans stood up straight and stretched himself. He looked at the barometer and smiled. "We'll have sunshine soon," he said.

"That'll be the day."

"It could happen."

Evans walked over and looked at the compass. "Five degrees to port," he said.

The man at the wheel began to swing the ship over.

Martin looked out the window at the whiteness. He thought of Duval. His name had not been mentioned since the service early that morning.

"What's the procedure when somebody dies aboard ship, when somebody disappears?"

"An investigation."

"Just a routine one?"

"Usually. It's different if they disappear and nobody sees them."

"What happens then?"

"Still an investigation; a little more so, maybe."

"What are you going to tell them?"

"Just what I know. Last anybody heard the Chief was out on deck. Then he fell overboard."

"I wonder what they're going to think happened."

"Nothing happened except that. What makes you think anything else happened?" Evans spoke sharply.

"I don't think anything different happened," said Martin. "It's what they'll think, that's all."

"This thing's happened before. They know what to do. They'll be routine."

"I hope so."

Evans looked at him a moment. Then he looked out the window.

Martin yawned and watched the small gray waves splatter against the bow. Then the snow was suddenly gone. Weather was like that here. A snowstorm would stop in several minutes. A gale could blow up and be gone in five minutes.

"There it is," said Evans.

"What?"

"Arunga, off the port bow."

Martin looked and saw, for the first time, the black bulky coastline of Arunga.

"See that cape?" asked Evans.

"Yes. That the port?"

"That's the port," Evans said happily. "Go down and see what shape the lines are in."

"How long before we'll dock?"

"Couple of hours."

"Fine." Martin went below. Outside on deck the wind was cool and direct. The air was clear and he could make out details of the island mountains.

One of the deckhands came out of the focs'le, the ship's dog with him. The dog sniffed the air suspiciously and then, satisfied, headed for the galley.

"Is that Arunga, Mate?" asked the deckhand.

"That's Arunga."

"I guess we really made it. I guess it was pretty close some of the time."

"I'll say. We had luck."

"That's no lie." The deckhand walked back to the galley. Martin examined the lines. They seemed to be in good shape. He walked to the afterdeck and checked the stern line: undamaged. He walked into the salon.

The passengers were talking loudly. Their baggage was piled on the deck of the salon and they were ready to go ashore.

"Somebody would think you people wanted to get off this boat," said Martin.

The others laughed. "We've enjoyed it, of course," said the Chaplain charitably. "But, we are, ah, land creatures, if you know what I mean."

"I thought it was pretty interesting," said Hodges. "Not everybody sees a wind like that."

"At least not many people get a chance to tell about it," agreed Martin.

Hodges and the Chaplain began to talk about the trip. Major Barkison, looking almost as young as he actually was, turned to Martin. "I hope there'll be no trouble about the accident."

"You mean Duval?"

"Yes. If I can be of any help at all just let me know. Tell Evans that, will you? I feel sure that nothing happened for which any of you could be held responsible." Having said this, the Major joined the Chaplain and Hodges.

Martin sat down. He knew what the Major thought. He knew what some of the crew thought, too: that Bervick had had something to do with Duval's death. No one would say anything about it, of course. The crew would be loyal to Bervick. Evans would pretend that the thought had never occurred to him. Of the passengers only the Major appeared to suspect anything. The Chaplain would never think of it. Hodges might.

"When are we docking?" asked Hodges.

"Around an hour or so."

"Isn't that marvellous," exclaimed Chaplain O'Mahoney. "I'm sorry," he added quickly. "We've all appreciated what you've done."

"I know how you feel," said Martin. "It's too bad we had to have so much excitement."

"That," said the Chaplain, "is life." There was no answer to this. Martin went into the galley and watched Smitty fixing supper.

"We going to Seward next, Mate?" asked Smitty.

"Some place like that. We'll have to go to drydock somewhere."

"Well, I want to get off somewheres. I don't like this stuff."

"That's too bad." Martin was getting tired of Smitty's complaints. He went slowly up the companionway to the wheelhouse.

Bervick and Evans were talking. They stopped abruptly when Martin entered.

"How're the lines?" asked Evans.

"Good shape."

"We'll be docking soon."

Martin looked out the window. Ahead of them he saw the string of tombstone-like rocks that marked the entrance. They were a little over five miles from the rocks.

Bervick opened one of the windows and the wind cooled the hot wheelhouse.

"Look," said Bervick, pointing at the sky.

"What do you see?" Martin asked.

"Gulls, lots of gulls. Can't you see them?"

Martin strained his eyes and with much effort he was able to see dark specks moving in the cloudy sky.

Evans looked at the sky, too. "Well, here we are," he said, almost to himself.

They drew closer and closer to the rocks of the entrance.

"We'll dock in about fifteen minutes," said Evans. "We'll be inside the harbor then anyway. You two go below and get the crew together. Remember we haven't got a guardrail."

"O.K., Skipper," said Martin. He and Bervick went below to the galley. The crew was gathered about the galley table. They were talking casually of the williwaw and somewhat less casually of Duval.

"Let's hit the deck," said Martin. "We going to tie up soon. Stand by on the lines."

The deckhands went out on deck; Martin and Bervick followed them.

Bervick took a deep breath. "When the weather's good it's really good here."

"It's appreciated anyway." They watched the men move about the deck, uncoiling lines, arranging the lines for the landing.

They entered the bay of Arunga.

The bay was several miles long. Mountains sloped down to the water. On the steep slopes were the buildings of the port and the army post. They were spaced far apart along the water edge. There were many brown, rounded huts and large olive-drab warehouses. There were cranes on the shore for unloading ships and there were many docks.

"Looks good," said Martin, "looks good. I never thought I'd be glad. . . ."

"Neither did I," said Bervick.

The ship glided at half speed through the nets. They were still over two miles from the docks.

"Is the radio out?" asked Martin.

"What? No, I don't think so. I don't think it is. No, I heard Evans tell the signalman to contact the shore."

"I'll bet they're plenty curious on shore."

"Because we haven't got a mast?"

"Sure, what did you think I meant?"

"I don't know. We're pretty late arriving."

"They know there was a williwaw. They probably knew it here all along."

The windows of the wheelhouse were opened. Evans leaned out of one.

"All ready to land?" he yelled.

Martin nodded.

"We're going to the East dock. Tie up on this end. Port landing."

Martin nodded. Evans disappeared from the window. Bervick went aft to handle the stern lines. Martin walked forward to the bow. He turned on the anchor winch.

"We'll put the bow line on the winch," he said to the deckhand who was handling that line.

The man tossed one end of his line over the revolving winch. When they docked he would draw the bow into shore with the winch.

A crowd was gathered on the dock. They were pointing at the ship and talking. Martin felt suddenly important. He always did when he was at the center of things. Every eye was on their ship. What had happened to them would become one of the many repeated stories of the islands. They were part of a legend now. The ship that had been smashed in a williwaw and had lost her Chief Engineer in a mysterious fashion.

Evans slanted the ship hard to port. They were headed for the dock. Martin saw that he was going to do one of his impressive landings. For a moment he hoped that Evans would foul up the landing. He didn't, though.

Just as they seemed about to hit the dock Evans swung the ship hard to starboard. Easily, gracefully she glided along parallel to the dock.

One of the crew threw the heaving line onto the dock. A man caught it and pulled their bow line out of the sea. Then he threw it over a piling.

Evans cut the engines off.

"Pull the bow in," Martin shouted to the deckhand beside the winch. Quickly the man obeyed. The ship stopped moving. Several officers who had been standing on the dock climbed aboard. Martin walked slowly toward the afterdeck. The sea gulls began to circle about the ship.

ii

"Handle that carefully, please." The Chaplain was worried about his baggage and he did not like the looks of the man who was placing it on the dock.

"O.K., O.K., Chaplain. I got it all right. Nothing's going to get broke."

"Thank you." Chaplain O'Mahoney shuddered as his duffel bag fell wetly into a puddle on the dock. Undisturbed, the man began to load the other passengers' baggage on top of his duffel bag.

The Chaplain buttoned his parka tightly at the throat. It was not particularly cold but he did not like the thought of being chilled.

He walked up and down the forward deck while the longshoremen began to unload cargo. Men were walking all over the ship, examining the stump of the mast and the other scars of the storm. Up in the wheelhouse he could see Evans talking with a group of officers.

He looked up at the dock from time to time. Chaplain Kerrigan was supposed to meet him at the dock. In the morning there was to be a meeting of all Chaplains; they were to discuss something or other, O'Mahoney was not sure what. He wished that Kerrigan would arrive soon.

Hodges and Major Barkison came out on deck.

"All ready to go ashore?" asked the Major.

"Just as soon as they get unloaded," said the Chaplain. "This is the first time I've been on Arunga."

"Is that right? Would you like me to give you a lift? My staff car'll be here soon."

"No thank you. Someone's supposed to meet me."

"Fine." The Major climbed up on the dock and Hodges followed him.

O'Mahoney watched them take their baggage off his now-soaked duffel bag.

"Chaplain O'Mahoney?" a voice asked.

He looked to his left and saw a long thin person coming toward him.

"Hello, Kerrigan," O'Mahoney said, and with great care he pulled himself up on the dock. He tried not to strain himself because of his heart.

"We were almost afraid we weren't going to have you for our meeting," said Kerrigan as they shook hands.

O'Mahoney laughed. "Well, I almost didn't get here."

Kerrigan looked at the ship. "No mast, I see. We were told that one of the nastiest williwaws they've ever had hit you people."

"Is that right? It was really terrifying, if you know

what I mean. Wind all the time. Waves so big you couldn't see over them. Oh, it was dreadful."

"How long did the storm last?"

"Two days at least. It was bad most of the time, of course."

"Well, we had a prayer meeting of sorts for you."

"With good results, even from a Protestant like yourself." They laughed.

"You all ready to go?" asked Kerrigan.

"Well . . ." O'Mahoney stood undecided. He looked at his duffel bag, blotched with water. "I'd better check with the Master of the ship before I go."

He looked around for Evans. Finally he saw him standing with a group of officers near the edge of the dock. They were talking seriously. O'Mahoney walked over to Evans.

"I'm about to go," he said. "I wondered if. . . ." Evans looked at him blankly. Then he seemed to remember.

"That's O.K., Chaplain. Go right ahead. They may get hold of you for this investigation tomorrow, but that's all."

"They know where to get me."

"I don't suppose you'll be traveling back with us?"

The Chaplain shook his head. "I think I'll fly," he said.

Evans smiled. He was really a pleasant young man, thought the Chaplain suddenly. He appeared a little abrupt at times but then he had many responsibilities. They shook hands and said goodbye and murmured that they would see each other again at Andrefski.

Some twenty or thirty people were on the dock now, examining the ship. Officers and enlisted men and sailors from the navy boats crowded about the ship.

The Chaplain found Major Barkison talking to a gray-haired Colonel.

"On your way, Chaplain?"

"Yes. My friend just met me. I'm going to be out near Chapel Number One, I think."

"Well, you know where I am, Adjutant's Office. Drop by and see me." The Major was cordial and distant.

"I certainly will. Good luck."

"Good luck, Chaplain." They shook hands. Then the Chaplain shook hands with young Hodges who had been standing near by. The Chaplain walked back to where Kerrigan stood waiting.

"Come on," said Kerrigan. "It's getting cold, standing around like this."

"Be right with you." The Chaplain picked his duffel bag up out of the puddle. He looked at the black water marks.

"What a shame," said Kerrigan. "I'll help you." Together they put the duffel bag in the back of Kerrigan's jeep.

O'Mahoney climbed into the front seat of the jeep and Kerrigan got in beside him, carefully shutting the plywood door. Kerrigan started the engine and slowly they drove down the dock.

The Chaplain took a last look at the ship as they drove by her. The crew was hosing down the decks and the longshoremen were closing the hatch.

"I'll bet you're glad to be off that boat."

O'Mahoney nodded. "You know, that trip took years, literally years off my life. I don't think that I'm the same person now that I was when I left Andrefski."

"How come?"

"Oh, the wind and all that. Fear, I suppose you'd call it. Somehow all the little things that used to bother me don't seem important now, if you know what I mean."

"That right?" Kerrigan looked at him with interest. "There must be something purging about being so near to death."

"I think so." The Chaplain sighed. "Jealousy and things like that. Being afraid to die and things like that. They seem unimportant now." The Chaplain said these things and meant them.

"It must have been a great experience. I understand one of the men was lost."

"That's right. Poor fellow fell overboard. He was a Catholic."

"That doesn't follow, does it?"

"What? Oh, no," the Chaplain laughed. "Just an accident."

"You know Worthenstein, the rabbi who was up here?"

O'Mahoney nodded, "Fine chap."

"Well, he got himself stationed in Anchorage."

"No!" The Chaplain was indignant. "I wonder how he arranged that. I don't like to be unkind but. . . ."

Kerrigan nodded, "I know what you mean." A truck came suddenly around a corner. Quickly Kerrigan pulled the jeep out of its way.

"My gracious!" exclaimed Chaplain O'Mahoney. "Watch where you're going."

*   *   *   *

Major Barkison went out on deck just before the ship docked. He did not like to admit it but he could barely wait to get off. He stood watching as they drew near to shore.

He felt slightly sick when he saw the bow of the ship heading straight into the dock. He saw a group of men standing on shore. If the one on the left moved within the count of three they would smash into the dock. . . .

He was forced to admire the way in which Evans swung the ship over.

Hodges joined him with the baggage. "I got everything here, Major."

"Good, good. You might toss it up on shore." A deckhand came, though, and took the baggage for them.

"Looks like everybody's down to see us."

The Major nodded. Several officers were waving to him. His friend, the Chief of Staff, an old army Colonel, was waiting for him on the dock.

Impatiently Major Barkison watched the deckhands as they made the ship fast. When they were at last securely moored to the dock, he looked up at the wheelhouse and asked, "Is it all right to go ashore, Mr Evans?"

"Yes, sir," said Evans, who was standing by one of the windows.

The Major and Hodges climbed onto the dock. They were immediately surrounded by a group of officers.

Major Barkison was quite moved at the concern they

showed. It seemed that the ship had been reported missing and that they had given up all hope of seeing him again. It was only an hour before that they had heard the ship had been sighted off the coast of Arunga.

The Colonel was especially glad to see him. "We were pretty bothered. You know how it is. I hadn't any idea who we could make Adjutant if anything happened to you. Joe, here, he applied for the job." The Colonel pointed to a short, stout Captain and everyone laughed except Joe. Major Barkison smiled to himself: Joe probably *had* asked for his job.

"You get seasick?" asked the Colonel.

"Certainly not," said the Major. "You know my iron stomach." The junior officers laughed at this bit of esoterica, and Major Barkison began to feel more normal.

"They tell me they lost one of the men."

"Chief Engineer. He fell overboard."

"What a shame. We heard a garbled report about it. I suppose it was too late to do any good when they picked him up."

"Well, they never did find out when he fell over."

"Really?" The Colonel was surprised. "That's a new one. Those things happen, of course."

"They certainly do." All the officers began to ask questions about the trip.

"I don't see how you had the nerve to take a boat out at this time of year," commented Joe admiringly.

"Well." The Major frowned and made his profile look like Wellington. "There were no planes flying," he said. "I had to get back. The General wanted my report and this was the only way I could come. It could have been worse," he added and he knew as he said it that he was sounding foolish to Hodges, if not to himself.

"We certainly appreciate that, Barkison. Not many people would have done it," said the Colonel.

Major Barkison was about to say something further when the Chaplain walked up to him to say goodbye. The Major spoke with the Chaplain for a few minutes. He liked O'Mahoney but Chaplains generally did not appeal to him. They exchanged goodbyes.

"Got some good news for you, Barkison," said the Colonel when the Chaplain had left.

"What is it?"

"You're been promoted, Colonel."

Major Barkison was very happy. The congratulations which flowed in around him made up for the fear in which he had spent the past few days.

"When did it come through?" he asked finally.

"Day before yesterday. I got something for you." The Colonel searched in one of his pockets and brought forth two silver Lt Colonel's leaves. "I'll pin them on," he said. He managed to get the Major's insignia off but his hands got cold before he could pin the new insignia on.

"Oh, hell," said the Colonel, handing the leaves to Barkison. "Put them on later."

"Thank you," said Barkison.

"Let's get out of here," said the Colonel. "We got two cars." He waved to two staff cars which were parked on the other end of the dock. Their drivers got into them and in a moment the cars were beside the ship.

"Here's Evans," said Hodges as Barkison was about to get into one of the cars.

"Oh yes, Mr Evans. Do you think you can come to my office sometime tomorrow? We'll talk over that investigation business."

"I certainly will, sir."

"And thank you for everything, Mr Evans. You did a fine job."

"Thank you, sir."

Barkison nodded and Evans walked away.

Barkison sat between the Colonel and Hodges in the back seat. For the first time he noticed the difference between being on land and on the sea. The steadiness of the land soothed him. He felt safe.

"You're giving us a party, aren't you, brother Barkison?"

"Certainly, Colonel. I've been saving up some liquor for a moment like this."

The Colonel laughed. "You dog, you knew all along

you were going to get this. I bet you were counting the days."

"Oh, not quite," said Barkison. He was thankful now that he was still alive. He felt like making a dramatic speech. He began to think of General Gordon and this made him think of his own immediate General.

"I hope the old man doesn't think I'm too late in getting back."

The Colonel shook his head. "Don't give it a second thought. He was glad to hear that you're still with us. The report could have waited."

"That's a relief," said Lt Colonel Barkison and he relaxed in his seat as the staff car took them quickly over the black roads to the Headquarters.

* * * *

Hodges helped put the baggage on the dock. Then he stood with the Major while the other officers asked questions. Hodges, as much as he admired the Major, could not help thinking that he was a bit of a poseur. He watched the Major as he talked of the storm. The Major was much too assured. From the way he talked one would have thought that he had brought the ship in.

Evans came over to say goodbye and Major Barkison was rather patronizing. Hodges wondered if he should be patronizing, too. He decided not.

"Goodbye, Mr Evans," he said. "We really appreciate what you did for us."

"Thanks. I'll probably see you around tomorrow."

"I hope so."

Evans walked back to the ship and Hodges joined the Major in the staff car.

"Well, Lieutenant," said the Colonel, "what do you think of your boss here getting promoted?"

"I'm certainly glad, sir."

"That's the spirit. Maybe you'll be, too." The Colonel chuckled.

Barkison was quiet, Hodges noticed. He seemed to be dreaming about something. Hodges could always tell when Barkison was daydreaming because his mouth would become very stern and he would look straight ahead, his lips occasionally moving.

"How was this guy," the Colonel nodded at Barkison, "how was he on the trip? I'll bet he was sick all the time."

"Oh, no, sir. I don't think he was sick at all." Hodges disliked higher ranking officers being playful.

The Colonel and Barkison began to talk about various things and Hodges looked out the window.

It was several miles to the Headquarters. It was several miles to everything around here.

The countryside, if it could be called that, was bleak and brown. There was no vegetation, only the spongy turf. Low hills sloped down into the water and beyond them the white mountains disappeared into the clouds.

Ravens and gulls were everywhere. Some of the younger officers had caught ravens, slit their tongues, and occasionally had taught them how to talk. Ravens made good pets.

"I wonder how the Chaplain's going to get back to Andrefski?" asked Hodges.

"I haven't any idea," said Barkison. "He'll probably fly. Are planes flying out of here now, Colonel?"

"Certainly. They have all along. Well, except for a few days last week."

Barkison smiled tightly. "Just when we wanted one, they stopped flying."

"It must have been a great experience for you," said the Colonel. "I'd give anything to have been in your shoes. That ship was really busted up."

"Yes, we took quite a knocking." Barkison looked away dreamily as though he were reliving those daring hours when he had stood on the bridge shouting orders to the men. Hodges thought this was very funny.

"I know the General thinks a lot of you for this. I heard him say so this morning at a staff meeting, which reminds me we've got a new Colonel in the Headquarters."

"Who is it?"

"Jerry Clayton. He was at the Point before your time."

"The name's familiar. What's he going to do here?"

"Well, this is just between us, Barkison, but I suspect. . . ." The Colonel lowered his voice and Hodges looked out the window.

The staff car drove up to a long building, rather complicated-looking because of its many wings. Hodges opened the door and they got out.

"I'll see you later, Hodges," said Barkison. "I've got to go in and see the old man. You'll be over at the club for supper, won't you?"

"Yes, sir. I'm going over there right now."

"I'll see you then." Barkison and the Colonel walked down a long dimly lit corridor to a door marked Commanding General.

Hodges went to his own office. This was a large room which he shared with three clerks and two Lieutenants. Only one of the Lieutenants was in the room when Hodges entered.

"Well, what do you know, here's the boy again," said the Lieutenant, grinning and shaking hands. "You don't look so bad. A little pale, but nothing that a dose of raisin jack won't cure."

"Well, you look plenty lazy." They insulted each other good-naturedly for several minutes. The other Lieutenant was in his middle twenties and a close friend of Hodges. They had gone to Officers' School together. The other Lieutenant was dark and handsome and constantly shocked at Hodges' desire for a military career. A desire which he usually referred to as "crass" or "gross."

"How's the office been?"

"Just about the same. I think our friend the Chief of Staff is going to get moved out."

"How come?"

"Well, they sent a new Colonel in and it looks like our politician friend is on his way out."

"I guess that's why he was down to meet us."

"Sure, he's winning friends all the time."

"Say, I'm hungry. Let's go over to the club."

"O.K., wait till I take care of this." The Lieutenant put some papers in his desk. "I wonder where that damn CQ is? Well, we'll go anyway."

They went outside and Hodges saw that his baggage

was gone. The driver had probably taken it over to his quarters. He was glad that he wouldn't have to carry it.

They walked silently along the black roads. Jeeps and trucks clattered by them. Men on their way to the theaters or cafeterias or recreation halls walked along the road. The twilight was almost as dark as the night.

The club was another long low complicated building.

Inside, it was warm and comfortable. There was a large living room with a fireplace and comfortable chairs. In here it was almost possible to forget that one was in the Aleutians.

Next to the living room was a bar and beyond that a dining room. Hodges and the Lieutenant went to the bar.

"Beer."

"Beer."

They got beer.

"Those little ships are pretty light, aren't they? I mean even in good weather they jump all over the place."

Hodges took a swallow of the bitter liquid. "I wouldn't know," he said at last. "I've never been in a boat like that in good weather."

"I guess that's right. Say, did you stop off at the Big Harbor?"

"We were there for a night."

"How was it? I never been there but I've heard a lot about the girls there. Got a lot of Canadians there."

"Well, they're all over fifty."

"That's not what I heard."

"That's what I saw anyway."

They drank their beer. "Come on," said Hodges when they had finished, "let's go in the dining room. I'm starved."

"Didn't they have food on that boat?"

"They had it but it was pretty hard to get down when you were jumping about like we were."

The dining room smelt of steak. They took a table in a corner, and a man took their order.

Barkison, wearing his new silver leaves, entered the dining room with the Colonel. They nodded to the Lieutenants who nodded back.

"Is that what you want to be? A guy like Barkison: more brass than brains?"

"Oh, he's not so bad. You just have to get to know him. He's done pretty well. He might even be a General before this is over."

"No war could last that long."

The waiter brought them their dinner. Hodges ate hungrily.

"By the way," said the Lieutenant, "I heard that a guy got killed on your boat. Mast hit him or something?"

"That's not quite right. He fell overboard."

"How did that happen?"

"I don't know. Nobody knows. He went out on deck to fix something and he never came back."

"You think he got the old push, maybe?"

"No, I don't," said Hodges and he spoke more sharply than was necessary.

"Well, don't get so excited. It wouldn't have been the first time. Was he a popular guy?"

"No, I don't suppose he was."

"That sounds mighty familiar to me."

"I think it was an accident, though," said Hodges and he said the words lightly, not making the mistake of sounding too interested as he had before.

"This is the toughest steak I ever ate," complained the dark Lieutenant.

"That's one of the horrors of war."

"It sure is." They finished their dinner.

Hodges thought of the night that the Chief had disappeared. He could remember himself building a house of cards. He could hear the Chief and Bervick arguing. Then they went out together and he had stayed inside building his house of cards. He had gone out on deck once. Duval had been sitting on the railing and Bervick was fixing the ventilator. Then he had gone back inside.

"Want some water?" asked the waiter, filling his glass, and Hodges thought of the splashing sound and of Bervick coming back into the salon alone.

"What's the matter with you?" asked the dark Lieutenant.

"Nothing's the matter with me. What's on at the show tonight?"

iii

Bervick came into Evans' cabin. It was seven o'clock and Evans was still asleep.

"Hey," said Bervick, and he shook him.

"What's the matter?" Evans sat up in bed.

"Nothing's the matter. Just thought I'd see if you were up."

"Well, I'm not up." Evans stretched out again in his bunk. For a moment he lay there quietly, his eyes half shut. He enjoyed the gentle rocking of the ship.

"Get me a cigarette," he said finally. Bervick felt in his pocket and brought out a crumpled pack. He took out a cigarete, lit it, and handed it to Evans.

"Thanks," grunted Evans. He inhaled the smoke comfortably. Then he began to think. When he awakened in the morning he always knew if something pleasant or unpleasant was supposed to happen to him. Today he felt would be a pleasant day.

"What you got on your mind?" Evans asked.

"Nothing, nothing at all."

"That's what I thought. What're you doing up so early?"

"Just messing around, that's all. I couldn't sleep."

"You never do sleep in the morning. You've probably got a guilty conscience."

"What do you mean?"

"Well," Evans looked at him a little surprised, "well, I don't know what I mean, do you?"

"How should I?"

"This isn't making much sense."

Bervick agreed. Evans looked at him thoughtfully. He had been acting strangely lately, ever since the Chief had disappeared. Evans wondered absently if Bervick might not have had something to do with Duval's death. He examined the idea with interest. Bervick might have hit him on the head with a hammer and then he might have dropped him overboard. That was not at all unlikely. Evans smiled.

"What's so funny?"

"Nothing, nothing at all. I was just thinking."

"What about?"

"I was thinking what a funny thing it would be if you'd knocked the Chief on the head and tossed him overboard."

"Well, I didn't," said Bervick. His voice was even. "Don't know that I wouldn't have liked to."

"It doesn't make much difference one way or the other," said Evans, quite sure now that Bervick had killed Duval. "It doesn't make no difference at all. He was better off out of the way. Guys've been knocked off before. Nicer people than the Chief have been knocked off."

"I thought about doing it a lot, but I didn't do anything to him. He just lost his balance."

"You saw it then?"

Bervick nodded slowly. "Yeah, I saw him fall off."

"Well, don't tell me any more about it. I don't want to know."

"What're you going to tell the investigating people?"

"That I don't know nothing about what happened, and that's what you're going to tell them, too."

"You think I should?"

"I sure do." Evans made smoke-rings. He was surprised at how easily he was able to take all this. He felt certain that Bervick had been responsible for the Chief's death. He should report what he knew but he would not. He would rather protect Bervick. Duval was dead now and he saw no reason why anyone else should be hurt.

"You know I didn't push him," said Bervick. He looked strained, Evans thought.

"O.K., then you didn't. I don't care."

"I just want you to get that clear. I didn't push him or do anything else. He just lost his balance."

"I believe you," said Evans, and he almost did.

"I don't want to talk about this any more. Is that all right with you?"

"Sure it is. You know what my report's going to be. Let's forget about it."

"Fine." Bervick looked better already, and Evans wondered if perhaps Bervick was telling the truth. Evans puffed on his cigarette. He was not curious to know what had happened and he would probably never know. It was Bervick's business, not his.

"Going to see the Major this morning?"

Evans groaned. "I suppose I have to." He got out of bed and shivered in the cold room. He always slept naked, even in winter. Quickly he dressed himself. Then he looked at himself in the mirror. He looked scrofulous. Evans was not sure what the word meant, but it had been going through his mind for several days and the sound of it was most descriptive. From time to time he would mutter the word to himself. Evans combed his hair and reminded himself again that he would have to get a haircut soon.

"Are you ready?" asked Bervick, who had been watching him impatiently.

"All ready." Evans put on his cap and they left the cabin and the wheelhouse.

One of the deckhands was out on deck trying to tack another piece of canvas over the hole where one of the forward ventilators had been. As Evans and Bervick went by him, he asked, "Say, Skipper, do you know what happened to the hammer? The one we keep in the lazaret."

"No, I don't. It was in there last I heard. You know anything about it, Bervick?"

"I used a hammer to fix the ventilator the other night. I stuck it back in the lazaret."

"Well, it ain't there now."

"You better look again," said Evans.

"It ain't there." The man turned back to his work and Evans and Bervick climbed up on the dock.

Evans chuckled and Bervick said nothing.

They walked past the warehouses and the docks. Bervick was very quiet and Evans did not bother him.

He looked at the sky and saw that the gray clouds were beginning to thin. Perhaps they would have a good day, one of those days when the sky was blue and the sun shone clearly. He watched the sea gulls dart and glide in the windless air.

Evans wondered what the Major would have to say about the investigation. He hoped there would not be too many questions. He was afraid Bervick would say the wrong thing.

A truck stopped for them and they got into the back.

"I don't think Barkison's going to be too much bother," said Evans. "I think he'll help us out."

"I hope so. Not that we've got anything to hide from him, much."

"Sure, that's right. We haven't got anything to hide."

The truck stopped at the Headquarters and they jumped out.

They entered a large well-lighted room, full of clerks and typewriters and file cases and all the necessary impedimenta of waging war.

Evans asked an effeminate-looking Corporal where he might find the Adjutant's office.

"Right down the hall, sir. First door on the left, sir." The man emphasized the "sir" in an irritating manner.

Evans and Bervick walked down the corridor. The anteroom to the Adjutant's office was smaller than the room they had just left. Several clerks and several Lieutenants had desks here. On the walls were charts of as many things as it was possible to chart or graph.

Evans noticed that one of the empty desks had the sign "Lt Hodges" on it.

"Can I help you, sir?" asked a clerk.

"Yes, I'd like to see Major Barkison."

"You mean *Colonel* Barkison."

"When was he promoted?"

"Well, he got it yesterday. You're the Master of the boat he was on, aren't you?"

"That's right."

"I think he's expecting you. Wait here please." The man went into the adjoining office and came out a moment later. "Colonel Barkison is busy right now. He'll see you in a few minutes. Why don't you sit down?"

"O.K." Evans sat in Hodges' chair and Bervick sat on the desk.

"Quite an office Barkison's got here," commented Bervick.

"Yeah, I'd go crazy in a job like this, though. He sits on his butt all day long."

"I'd sure like to make the money he makes."

"You could make more fishing."

"Could be." They waited for fifteen minutes. Then Lt Hodges came out of Barkison's office.

"How are you?" he greeted them. "You can go in now."

"Thanks."

Lt Colonel Barkison was sitting behind his desk, his mouth firm and his jaw set as he shuffled some papers. He looked up as they came in. Evans and Bervick did not salute and Evans was not quite sure whether Barkison was disappointed or not.

"Good morning, Evans, Bervick. How's your boat today?"

"Just fine, Colonel."

"Good." Barkison did not invite them to sit down and that irritated Evans.

"About this investigation. . . ." Barkison began. He paused and seemed to be thinking. Then he said, "I've been appointed Investigating Officer."

"Is that right, sir? I thought they would hold the investigation at Andrefski."

"Normally they would, but you're not going back there. We just got word from Andrefski that you're to proceed straight to Seward for repairs." Barkison smiled. "Maybe you'll even get to Seattle."

"That's the best news I've heard," said Evans, delighted. Bervick agreed with him.

"So," Barkison frowned, "I've been made Investigating Officer." He paused again, then he confided, "I'll tell you what I'm going to do. I'll take statements from you two and some others who might have seen Duval. We'll do all that tomorrow. From what I've already gathered I feel that nothing new will turn up. So I can tell you *now* that I'm going to report plain accident in line of duty."

"I'm glad it'll be as simple as that," said Evans, not knowing what else to say.

"I feel you've had enough trouble without an unpleasant investigation," said Barkison and Evans noticed that he was careful not to look at Bervick.

"Thank you, sir."

"Don't mention it. I'm quite appreciative of what you, ah, did. I'm not quite sure in my mind, however, that it was a wise thing to do, to take a ship out in such bad weather."

Evans was surprised and a little angry. "What do you mean, Major, I mean Colonel?"

"Nothing at all, except that some might say, now mind you I don't, but some might say you showed bad judgment."

"I don't know what you're talking about, sir. You insisted on the trip. I said that we were taking a chance, that was all." Evans tried to keep the anger out of his voice.

"I quite understand, Mr Evans," said Barkison coldly, beginning to shuffle his papers again. "I shall see you tomorrow."

"Yes, sir." Bervick saluted and Evans did not as they left Barkison's office.

"Well," said Bervick when they were outside the Adjutant's office, "there goes that medal of yours."

"I'd like to knock that little bastard's head in," said Evans with feeling. "Did you hear him say I showed bad judgment?"

"Well, he had to pass the buck; I mean, it would look bad if people heard he insisted on taking this trip in such bad weather. He just wants to cover himself."

"That man sure changed from what he was on the boat."

"He's just acting natural."

Hodges came into the outer office as they were about to leave.

"What's new?" he asked.

"Not a thing," said Evans.

"How long you going to be around?"

"A few more days, maybe. We're going to Seward."

"So I heard. That's a good deal."

"I'll say."

"Well, I'll be seeing you around," said Hodges. He

looked at Bervick a moment and he seemed about to say something. Then he decided not to. "See you," he said.

They said goodbye and went outside.

"What's the matter with Junior?" asked Evans. "He looked at you sort of queerly."

"He's got too much imagination, I guess."

"Is that it?"

"That's it." Bervick smiled.

The sky was blue and clear now and the sun shone on the white mountains. They walked back to the ship.

We know you don't read just one kind of book. | That's why we've got all kinds of bestsellers.